MW00877598

Christopher Coleman

# Chapter 1

"Hi Sharon. It's me. It's Dominic."

The thing that used to be Sharon shows no glint of recognition, and I wonder if it can hear me at all. Her external ears gone, and as she approaches, bringing me as close to the creature as I've been since the event happened a couple of months ago, can see only the tiniest of orifices on the sides of her head. They appear almost reptilian, like those of an ashen crocodile, a comparison made more apropos by the cold blackness of her eyes.

But the thing seems to hear my words, giving a cock of its head, like a beagle who's just been asked a question.

"I should have been here with you when it happened. And I'm sorry for that. I'm so sorry for everything." I pause, thinking of Naia. "Some of them things you never even knew about."

It is guilt that has brought me here, to my home of fourteen years, by way of the refrigerated box truck that sits parked outside in my driveway, the engine running, my new companions—who are now only four in number—still screaming my name, warning me to leave. But I've made the decision to follow through on my plan, a plan I finalized on my way here and which sounded in my head something like this: if my wife was still here at our home, alive somehow, I would tell her everything, all about Naia and the affair, as well as the weeks I'd spent at the student union and later the diner. And then, once the plates stopped flying, I would try to convince her to come with us. She would hate me for a while, forever maybe, but she would be with me, under my protection. And alive.

On the other hand, if she was dead, or not here at all, I would turn back to the truck immediately and go with the group. I would be broken and distraught, and my heart would no doubt be overflowing with culpability, but there would be nothing to do at that point other than go on, so that's what I would do.

But there was a third possibility to prepare for. If Sharon had turned into one of them, had become one of the victims of the snow, I would stay. It was a conditional suicide mission, of course, since I now know of their strength and had witnessed the violent things they did to Naia and Alvaro. And it was also a mission I had not revealed to my traveling party.

Sharon is only six feet from me now, maybe less, and there is a familiar smell that I realize is the same one that came from the Thai restaurant where Alvaro was killed. I hadn't placed the crab as the source of the odor at the time—not with all the spoiled food left over in the kitchen—but I have no doubt about it now. It's a chemical smell, something close to ammonia.

She's now only a couple of feet away, but I stand my ground. Her skin is so white and her eyes so black she looks like a human-sized version of a classic cartoon ghost.

Until she opens her mouth.

Inside, past the thing's white lips, instead of the black abyss found in the eyes of the crab, there is the color of flesh and gum. Teeth and tongue. All the pink and viscous characteristics of her pre-crab self.

Sharon closes her eyes and the black pools disappear beneath eyelids as white as the snow that created them. She opens them again, this time only halfway, and then, without even the

slightest twitch of a warning, she thrusts her body towards me, raising her naked white arms above her as she comes, looking like some kind of crazed albino chimpanzee.

I close my eyes to accept her attack, awaiting the crash of this not-quite-human body against mine, preparing to fulfill my morbid plan. Just before it reaches me, before its bleached skin connects with the layers of clothing covering my body, I have an absent thought of the afterlife, about what the universe has in store for my soul once the next thirty seconds or so ends.

And then comes the explosion.

The sound of the blast deafens me for a moment, and my first thought is that I've already begun my entry into that afterlife that I've just conjured. The blast was the sound of God's voice, perhaps, as He prepared to explain to me that I have no right to His kingdom.

It takes me only seconds, however, to realize I'm still a part of this earth, awakened by the contents of the crabs' innards collapsing on and all around me. As I had known from the incident inside the Thai restaurant, when the crab was crushed by the freezer door, the insides of the things appeared just like those of any normal human—red and purple and sticky—and I'm coated in a shower of blood and bone and brain, as well as the unique additive of vanilla skin.

Sharon's torso propels forward and lands on top of me, and, instinctively, I catch it in my arms before releasing it almost instantly, hurling it to the side with a gasp, watching in horror as the lump of flesh thumps to the floor. The headless corpse of my wife now spouts a geyser of blood from between the shoulders across the foyer and into the carpet of the living room. Absurdly, I think of how badly Sharon had wanted hardwood in that room, and how distraught she would be at this mess.

I've lost the ability to breathe, to blink, and as I stare at the dead creature below me, I'm suddenly baffled by its demise. Did I somehow destroy it through some telepathic feeling of love or blame or fear? Was what remained of the crab's intellect incapable of co-existing with the deluge of emotions occurring inside of me, causing it to explode?

And then I look up and see her. It's Danielle, standing tall, her eyes wide and her face nearly as white as the one she's just destroyed. Beside her, butt down and barrel in her left fist, is the shotgun that she's brought with her from the diner. It's the same one she had pointed at me from the street on the day Naia and I left the student union of Warren College and ended up in the parking lot of Balmore Plaza. Naia had gone to scope out the Thai restaurant, and I had taken to investigating a box truck that sat out in front of the diner where Danielle worked. Within seconds the shotgun was on me, Danielle protecting the contents of the truck with attitude and buck shot.

My feelings about what has just occurred a foot or two inside my home, about what Danielle has just done to my wife, are beyond my analysis, and I can only remain frozen in place, a statue of fear and sickness and uncertainty.

"What the hell are you doing, Dominic?" Danielle asks, her words slow and wary as she stays focused on the corpse at my feet. She takes a deep breath and then looks up at me finally. "Why did you do this? Why did you come inside here? You heard us. You must have seen her...it. Look at it, Dominic. There was nothing you could do."

"I told Tom not to wait for me," I answer, my voice low and robotic, and I force myself to avoid Danielle's eyes. "I was clear about that."

"If you thought that's what Tom would do—what I would do—just leave you to die, then you don't know us at all. But I guess that's the truth isn't it? You don't know us."

Danielle pauses, waiting for some rebuttal.

"I was out of the truck the second I saw that thing in the window. Before you even stepped foot inside. No suicides, Dom. Not at this point in the story."

In spite of myself, I turn my head away in shame. Hearing the word 'suicide' as applied to me is unsettling in a way I wouldn't have imagined.

"People have been murdered, Dominic. Friends of mine. Tom's son. People who didn't deserve to die but did anyway. And now you want to just throw yourself on the pyre? I don't think so."

"I should be the one lying here, not her. I was the one who cheated. I was the one who was off with my...It should have been me. I should have protected her."

Danielle sighs, and I can imagine the glaze of sympathy that comes over her face. "Protecting her from what, Dom? The snow? What would you have done differently? You wouldn't have known. We still don't really know what happened, except that the snow fell, and, if you happened to be outside in it at the time, you...well, you know the rest. But tell me honestly, Dominic, would you have kept your wife from going outside?"

I know Danielle is right. I couldn't have kept Sharon from enjoying the snow even if I had wanted to. And why would I have wanted to? "We could have gone together," I say, answering another question altogether.

"I know Dom, and death would have meant an end to the pain you're feeling. But that pain will lessen—it will—and in the meantime, with the life you still have, you can use it to keep her in your memories."

I smirk and give a gentle scoff, finally meeting Danielle's eyes. "Pretty smart for a waitress," I say, continuing a running joke.

Danielle smiles. "And besides, the main reason you can't die is because we need you. Who knows what we're going to run into out there? You menfolk had gone out of style there for a while, but you're suddenly back in fashion."

I give a full laugh now, and then a single tear falls down my cheek, followed by a full on weeping session. I sit on the floor with my back against the door, crying into my hands, the smell of my dead wife's altered body heavy in the air. Danielle doesn't say a word. When the tears finally end, I take a deep breath and say, "So where do we go from here?"

"We know things we didn't before," Danielle answers, not missing a beat. "About the event that caused this. And we have a pretty good idea it was our government that was behind it. Or at least some kind of shadow government working in secret. I guess I'd like to believe that. I mean, who else has tanks?"

"I'm not sure we *know* any of that, but let's say we do. Let's say Terry and Stella were telling us the truth about what they knew. What does that mean?"

"It means we can do something to stop them. It means we have an obligation to stop them."

I shake my head, confused. "Stop them? It's been done. Whatever caused this, whatever brought the snow and the crabs, it doesn't really matter anymore. It's already happened. By all accounts, it's happened everywhere."

"Those radio reports were lies, Dominic. You know that. You heard Terry and Stella. Those reports were just part of the experiment."

"We *don't* know that for sure either. Whatever plan Terry and Stella were a part of was obviously not the real plan, not fully, so we have no idea what's true or not. It could be that the reports were right after all. It could be the world is, for all intents and purposes, over." I've regained my sense of the moment now and have, at least temporarily, accepted the death of my wife, whose body still lay at my feet, the pool of blood at the base of her neck and shoulders enormous.

"So what then, Dom? You're just going to give up? Should I just go ahead and take your head off too?" Danielle raises the gun to her shoulder and stares at me through the sight. "This what you want?"

In a way, it is what I want, even though I know Danielle's dramatic display is just for show. But what is there to do now? The world has been changed beyond repair, at least the world that we can see from here, and it's a world now inhabited by murderous crabs and some demented military force.

I hear the front door open behind me, and I turn my head to see Tom standing at the threshold. He surveys the scene with a look of sympathy, and then gestures toward Danielle to lower the gun.

"They've been keeping their distance so far," Tom says, "but they're closing the perimeter. We have to go soon if we're gonna. Can't leave Terry and James out there with no weapon. Are you ready, Dominic?"

Tom has the demeanor of a grandfather and the gravitas of a general, and all I can do is nod.

Tom looks to Danielle. "Weren't gonna shoot Dom were you, Danny?"

Danielle cocks her head and shrugs. "Guess we'll never know."

Tom snorts a laugh and gives a twitch of his head, gesturing toward the truck. I follow him out to the stoop and instantly see the closing circle of crabs to which Tom just alluded, their alabaster bodies nearly featureless against the backdrop of the snowy landscape. The closest one is still probably thirty yards away, but my former subdivision is a closely packed cul-de-sac of houses and shrubs and trees, and with a blanket of snow covering all of it, it's hard to know where any one of the white monsters might be hidden. There could be one crouched behind a parked car, or maybe camouflaged next to a downspout, and we would never see it until it was too late.

And though we've been able to observe them periodically over the last several weeks, their movements are still somewhat unknown. We know they have the potential to be violent, of course—I've already seen two people killed in front of my eyes—and when they did kill, they were ferocious in the way they devoured the bodies, tearing at the flesh with their teeth and hands, continuing to maul the corpse long after death had come to the victim.

But exactly when and why they attack is still somewhat unpredictable. It seems proximity plays a critical part, but the exact distance at which they are triggered remains a mystery. And perhaps sound and movement play a role as well. They appear incredibly curious by sounds and actions that don't follow a regular pattern of behavior.

I step up into the passenger seat of the truck and move to the middle, allowing Danielle space to move in beside me. Tom reclaims the driver's seat; the engine is still running. Neither James nor Stella, who are both seated in the back, say a word.

I look over at the dashboard and note the gas gauge, which is somewhere between a quarter tank and empty.

Tom doesn't look at me, but he seems to read my mind. "I guess before we can save the world, we're gonna have to find some fuel."

Danielle closes the passenger door and Tom immediately shifts the truck into reverse, allowing it to roll gently out to the street.

"There's a station a couple miles up near Turnberry, just off 2."

"Don't know where that is, but I'll follow your directions."

I nod and point straight ahead.

Tom shifts the truck into drive and eases us onto the freeway.

I look up to the clear sky above us and the sun shining brightly.

# Chapter 2

It hasn't snowed in days, and as we head north towards the city, with every mile that passes, the accumulated snow on the ground seems to thin. I have no way of knowing if it's due to the distance were putting between ourselves and College Valley, or if the weather has just improved, but every few minutes I throw a glance towards the odometer, tracking the miles.

"I need to know that you'll be able to do this with us," Danielle says from beside me. Hers are the first words anyone has spoken in twenty minutes, and I turn to see the side of her face pressed against the passenger door window; she seems to be staring up at the clouds in the distance.

"Do what?" I ask.

She turns her head toward me slowly. "Whatever it is we'll need to do to survive. I don't think I got confirmation from you back at the house, and I need to know you're with us."

I look away from Danielle, back towards the front of the truck. "I'm good. I've made peace with...what happened. You made a lot of sense about life or whatever."

"I'm not just talking about that. I'm glad you're feeling better, but you used us. You used us in order to leave the diner so that we could bring you to your house. But you didn't tell us of your full intentions. I understand why you did it, but it was still a violation of our trust."

"I wasn't completely honest with you, I'll admit that, but I didn't use anyone. We voted to leave the diner. And I seem to recall that you were in my camp from the start."

Danielle doesn't retort, and instead turns back to the window to continue her sky-gazing. "I *am* sorry about your wife, Dominic. Just in case I never said."

I swallow hard and feel the flood form behind my eyes again. "How far have we gone, Tom?"

I ask the question as a distraction. I already know it's been thirty-eight miles since we left my house and the wreckage of my former life. We passed the last of the county's businesses two miles back, and are now beyond the furthest point any of my companions have explored since the blast.

The two-lane stretch of highway is deserted, and has·been for the entire trip, other than the occasional crab crouched low on the side of the road, its shoulders pointing high above its head like a bat. Their gazes always seem to follow the truck as we pass, their eyes somehow never leaving mine, like one of those old posters where the stare of the subject would fixate on you no matter where you walked in the room.

"About thirty-five miles," Tom answers. "We're only 'bout ten miles from the county line."

Whereas Warren County is small and secluded, surrounded on three sides by water, the neighboring county of Maripo is a bustling suburb, a closer representation to the capital city bordering it to the north. It's also the home of Stella and Terry's employer, a vaguely labeled chemical engineering firm who, according to Stella, sent the two scientists to Warren to observe what was ostensibly to be only a psychological experiment, but instead turned out to be the disaster we're faced with now.

"This is your neck of the woods, right Stella." I say with a hint of contempt.

Since the moment Stella first revealed she and Terry were privy to the fatal experiment of Warren County, our interrogation of her has been steady, and Terry's demise back on the exit ramp at the hands of a mysterious army colonel has only enhanced our questioning. But the few details she's offered since the diner have been inconsequential. Still though, I feel like there's more she's not telling.

"I...yes, though not quite. Our laboratory is about fifteen minutes from here. Across the Maripo River Bridge and then just—"

"Holy Jesus!" It's James, and his voice is breathy and shocked. "What is that?" He's looking straight ahead, over my shoulder from his position in the back seat.

I follow his eyes through the windshield and see it immediately, a blanket of pale gray rising from the ground at the base of the Maripo River Bridge. We're still almost a mile from the bridge, but there is no mistaking the wall that's been constructed there; it's at least ten feet high, rising toward the sky like the façade of a skyscraper.

Tom continues to drive toward the white wall, no doubt thinking the same thing I am, that he's not seeing it properly, that it's some trick of the sky and landscape that's creating the illusion of a barrier.

But another hundred yards removes any doubt that the image is real. The wall is there, perhaps even higher than my initial ten-foot estimate, and it spans the entire width of the bridge, extending across the road and buttressing against the reinforced concrete traffic barriers on both sides of the highway.

Tom stops about a quarter mile short of the bridge and puts the truck in park. "Any suggestions?"

"Why would they do this?" James asks.

"It's like they've set up some type of quarantine area," Stella adds, her voice sounding as genuinely surprised as I would expect from someone not privy to any details.

"There are no soldiers though. No military or police presence at all. Wouldn't they have a tank or something, like back at the exit ramp?"

"What do you think, Stella," I say, "Where's the rest of the colonel's friends."

Stella scoffs, and I can feel her frustration behind me. "How long is this type of questioning going to go on?" Her voice is pitched, indignant, but I don't turn around.

"I suppose until we get answers," I reply.

"Well then I guess it's going to be for the rest of our time together, because I don't have any. Not about this anyway. I've told you everything I know about what was supposed to happen with the experiment. At least everything that I was told, which was obviously less than Terry."

"James is right, though," Tom says, ignoring the growing spat between Stella and me. "If they was really serious about keeping us from leaving, they'd have done more than throw up this wall. My guess is they ain't got the manpower to guard every exit road out of here."

Warren County is essentially a peninsula, attached to the mainland of the state to the west, and surrounded by water otherwise. And there are only three roads out, two of which are via bridges: the Maripo River Bridge at which we are currently, and the Howard Steeple Bridge at the south end of the county. Both of these bridges span water wide enough that a fit person could never swim them in perfect weather, and certainly not in freezing conditions like these.

"Then we'll head west along the river until we reach Hambleton," James suggests. "From there we'll take 7 out of town."

The other exit is west along the peninsula, the route James just suggested.

"I'd expect there'd be a roadblock there as well. And I have a feeling that might be the route where they've congregated their manpower."

"Why do you think that?" Stella asks, and a sense of suspicion activates in me once again.

"Just a hunch, really, but I'm guessing they figured if they blocked off the bridge with a wall too high to climb and too wide to get around, anyone who still wanted out would be forced to try another route, the most obvious being the one James just talked about. But even if they do block the road out of Hambleton, they can't block off the whole town, so I expect they're monitoring the road along the way and we'd meet some company before we ever got that far."

"What about south?" Danielle asks.

Tom shrugs. "That's the Steeple Bridge. Assume it would be like this 'un. Choked off at the source. And I don't think we got the gas to get there anyhow."

The gas station where we stopped on the way from my house had no working pumps, but we were lucky to find a couple of full containers in the garage. It's not a scenario we could necessarily depend on again.

"So maybe Dominic had the right idea after all," Danielle says, her voice loud and slightly panicked. "Maybe we should just throw ourselves at the feet of these crab things. Or shoot ourselves in the head and get it over with."

"Not saying that, Danielle," Tom assures, "just being honest about the situation."

"Let's take a look," I say, nodding toward the passenger door, encouraging Danielle to open it. She frowns and pushes open the door, and I follow her down to the thin layer of snow that now covers the asphalt. It's still pretty cold outside, but not anything like it was just a few weeks earlier when Naia and I were still holed up in the student union of the college. It seems like three lifetimes ago that I was there, bickering with her about whether or not to leave, about whether to brave the weather and the white beasts that lingered outside.

The crabs.

They had come only sporadically back then, showing up every couple of days, two or three at a time. That was until that last day when the sun returned and we made the decision to leave. Then there had been dozens. Attacking us like the cannibalistic monsters they turned out to be. It was that day that I knew the world had truly ended.

But we had managed to escape, fleeing the snow-covered campus of Warren Community College, sprinting across the quad until we were outside the college grounds and in the parking lot of Balmore Plaza, the shopping center that bordered the school to the east.

But that was the final stop for Naia. Before she ever had the chance to start again, to begin a new existence with the group in the diner, the crabs that had been waiting at the entrance of the Thai restaurant were on top of her, tearing out her insides with their bare hands.

It should have been me, of course, who went to investigate the Thai restaurant, the one who opened the door unexpectedly, only to be disembowelled by the proprietors inside who had turned with the snow.

But, once again, it wasn't me. It wasn't me at the restaurant and it wasn't me at home with my wife on that Sunday afternoon in May when the snow began to fall. My flaws have saved my life. My improprieties and cowardice and lack of principle are the only reason I'm still alive today.

And the truth is, despite my concessions to Danielle in my own foyer a couple of hours earlier, I don't really want to live anymore, and the guilt and loneliness that are promised in my future continue to rage. But I'm going to live anyway. I'm going to give it the effort at least, if only for the sake of the two women I've murdered.

I walk to the base of the bridge and stare up at the absolute unscalability of the wall in front of me. It's concrete in construction and looks similar to the noise barriers often seen along the highway, the ones backing against housing subdivisions to spare them the constant blare of passing traffic. The sides of the wall extend beyond the width of the road, blocking the entire view of the bridge from this distance and making it impossible to walk around and onto the bridge from the street.

I walk over to one of the guardrails that meets the base of the wall, and I can see beyond it the drop off to a steep hill that slopes down to a row of houses on the water. It looks to be at least a fifteen-foot rise from the bottom of the hill to the street, which means there will be no walking to the side of the bridge from the bottom and then climbing onto it from an angle.

The only way out of Warren County in this direction is on the water.

"That don't look too promising," Tom says, now standing beside me, following my gaze down the hill. "If you was thinking what I was."

"Yeah, it's what I was thinking."

"What are we going to do down there? We won't be able to get on the bridge from there." It's Stella, and beside her is James. Danielle walks up seconds later to complete the huddle at the base of the bridge.

"The way I see it," I say, "we have two options, and neither of them seems all that great."

Everyone stays silent, waiting for me to complete the idea.

"And I guess the option we decide to go with really depends on what our goals are."

"What does that mean?" Stella asks. "Goals?"

"Well, I mean, is our goal just to survive as long as we can? Hang out in this wasteland and hope someone from outside of this nightmare eventually comes to our rescue? A miracle helicopter or something. Or is our goal to keep going? To try and get as far as we can from this place, even if that means taking some big risks?"

The group is quiet again, this time pondering the options.

"What do you think, Dom?" It's Tom, and his eyes are soft, genuine, earnestly interested in my guidance.

"Of course I want to survive," I say without hesitating.

"Really?" Danielle asks, "Should that be obvious to us?"

The jab is fair, and I let it stand without responding. "But I also want to find out what happened. And to do that, in my opinion, we need to get out of here. And the closest exit out of here is the other side of the river."

Stella closes her eyes and begins to shake her head.

"What?" I ask. "Why the dismissive head shake?"

"Getting to the other side of the river doesn't guarantee you'll get answers."

"No? Isn't that where Dramatech is or whatever your company is called?"

"The name of the company is Drumbard and Wallace Technologies, and it's several miles past the bridge, which, I'll remind you, is blocked at the moment by the Great Wall of Warren. And even if you were somehow able to get us there, across the bridge and then to D&W, do you really think that you'll be able to just saunter right up and speak to the principles there? Especially if they are the ones behind all of this?"

I give Stella's concerns the proper consideration before replying. "No, probably not. But you might be able to."

Stella scoffs, her eyes wide and disbelieving. "I'm here too! Why would I be able to do that?"

"I'm sure you have your badge or whatever credentials you need to get inside the building."

Stella rolls her eyes and gives a quick quiver of her head, a signal that I have no idea what I'm talking about, which, in fairness, I don't.

James starts to laugh. "Inside the building? What are you talking about? That's the plan? Have you looked around? It's the middle of summer and there's snow on the ground. The world is over. I want to get out of this town too, but what makes you think there's anything for us across that bridge." He holds an extended arm out to the shores of the opposite bank.

"It's all white as far as any of us can see. Snow and snow and more snow. And can't you see them moving over there? Because I can. Hopping around like overgrown arctic rabbits, just lying in wait?"

James starts to laugh harder now.

"I think it's a possibility. That's all."

"Or it's a possibility that the fucking world has come to an end, and we'll spend the rest of our lives being hunted by ghosts? Except worse than ghosts, because even though they look like ghosts, they don't pass through you when they touch you, they tear out your goddamn kidneys!"

"That's all now, James," Tom says, his voice low and steady. "We all know the situation."

James begins to speak again and Tom snaps his head toward him; the diner owner's face remains calm and comforting, but there's a threat in his eyes that keeps James quiet.

"If you have a plan, James," I say without sarcasm, "I'm willing to hear it. I'm sure we all are." I hold James' stare until he shakes his head quickly and then turns and walks back to the truck in a huff.

We all watch James until he reaches the vehicle and slides back into the passenger seat, and then Tom looks back to me and says, "So you want to leave Warren County. Sounds like an idea to me. How we gonna do that?"

I nod toward the row of homes at the bottom of hill, which are a mixed tableau of modern-day mansions and sixties era ramblers; the latter, no doubt, belonging to older citizens who have lived on the coast for years and have had no interest in entertaining the barrage of offers thrown their way from wealthy investors. This is the place they've lived for most of their lives, the place where they've raised their families, made their livings, and intended to die. And it would seem at first glance, they realized their dreams in full.

Despite the variance in home sizes, however, the lots all seem to be spaced rather evenly in a horseshoe shape around the curve of the shoreline, with only a few precious yards of space between them. "You see these waterfront homes here?" I ask rhetorically.

Tom nods.

"Every one of them has a pier, which means most of them have boats."

Tom nods and then squints in confusion. "Don't see many boats though."

Tom's right: most of the piers are empty, and the few boats that are still docked seem to mirror the conditions of the houses; which is to say, the mansions have yachts, and the dated homes have old fishing boats which, even from a distance, display their weathering and fading paint.

"Don't suppose you'll have much luck with those yachts. No sensible person would leave keys to any beautiful boats like that inside. Probably do better with that Sea Nymph out yonder. 'Bout, uh, ten houses down, I'd say. See it?"

Tom points to a small fishing boat with a silver hull and pistachio green interior. Unlike the fancy yacht docked at the pier of the house beside it, the Sea Nymph has an outboard motor that, if it starts at all, will need every ounce of horsepower to move the five of us to the other side of the river. But we're not entering a regatta; we just need something to get us across.

"I think that might be the winner, Tom," I say, and I can almost feel Stella's incredulity bubbling beside me.

"That thing?" Stella asks finally, her tone tempered, but I'm sure that's only for Tom's sake.

"Do you have experience with boats, Dom?" Danielle asks.

"Not really, but we're not heading to Barbados. We just need to cross a mile, mile and a half of water. Still water at that. That's one silver lining of these freezing temperatures—they slow down the current."

"Dom's right," Tom says, "don't need to be a sea captain to take a motorboat across a river. And I've got plenty of hours on the water if need be."

"I think we might be needing," Stella jabs, and then grins over at me.

"But I would recommend that if this is to be our decision, we should get going with it. Whether it be that Nymph or sumpin' else, we should get down there and see if we can get one to start. And even if you do get the Nymph going, it wouldn't hurt to check the ignitions of some of those big boys either. If the keys are there, I think we'd all rather go in style."

"I think maybe only two of us should go down at first," I say, "and then, if we can get one going, we'll give a signal to whoever stays behind. Who's with me? Danielle?"

Danielle purses her lips and cocks her head, a gesture indicating flattery that she'd been recruited so quickly for the mission. She nods.

"Shall we then?"

"We shall."

I hop the guardrail and begin to make my way down the steep embankment that leads from the road and bottoms out into a small clump of tall trees that rise up above the freeway, naturally blocking the view of the houses from the road. Danielle follows right behind me.

The footing on the hill isn't treacherous exactly, but each step requires concentration; a sprained ankle wouldn't be the end of the world at this point, but it wouldn't be helpful either.

And then, despite my focus on the descent, something above and behind me stops me in my tracks midway down the hill. Whether it was because of a faint sound, one that didn't quite register consciously, or, perhaps, from some primitive, extra-sensory instinct of "being-watched," I feel compelled to turn back to the bridge. And when I do, I see them instantly.

There are at least a dozen of them, crabs, standing atop the side barrier of the bridge that faces us, their bodies hunched down like gargoyles, their bare white feet wedged between the bottom railing and the top of the concrete partition. Their knees knife straight out over the water, as if they're poised to jump, and though they remain virtually motionless from their necks down, their eyes follow our every move, their heads shifting constantly, keeping Danielle and I in the proper frame at all times.

I want to gag with fear, but I put a hand to my mouth to stifle any noticeable reaction. I turn back to the hill and see Danielle placing one foot carefully in front of the other. She hasn't seen the crabs or my reaction, and I suddenly feel a responsibility to keep both from her.

I return my focus to the hill, and the moment we reach the bottom and start towards the neighborhood, I keep her centered on the houses in front of us, feigning a bit of confusion about which home had the boat that we've decided is the best candidate for our journey. "I can't remember if it was the eighth or ninth house."

"Follow me," she says. "I've got it."

I fall in behind Danielle and follow her towards the house, jogging lightly as we go, and I can't help but look back to the bridge one more time. I can see Tom and Stella watching us from their place next to the wall, only a few yards from where the crabs are on the opposite side, and I give them a thumbs up, which Tom alone acknowledges by holding up an open hand. I then swallow and look over to the line of crabs, which have now doubled in size atop the railing. They look like a murder of crows, or, perhaps more aptly, seagulls.

We reach the tenth house from the bridge and I return my concentration to the mission, pushing through the picket gate and immediately venturing out to the back yard and onto the pier. The Sea Nymph bobs gently by the pier, meekly fighting against its mooring, and now that I'm only a foot or two from the small fishing boat, I can see that its even older than I suspected—it's thirty years old if it's a day—and uglier than a rusty trash can. But all the parts seem to be in place, and, most importantly, it's easily big enough to hold the five of us.

My concern, however, rests on getting it started, which, even if we can, its dependability once we're on the water is still a question. Getting stranded halfway across the Maripo River a year ago was an inconvenience; today it would be a death sentence.

"Listen," I say, studying the interior of the boat, "I think Tom may have had the right idea. I think we should see if one of these other, uh, shall we say more modern boats, has their keys in the ignition."

"Why? Is this old girl beneath you?"

"I'm not confident she *will* stay beneath me, that's the problem."

Danielle chuckles and then looks the boat over sympathetically. "I think it's kind of beautiful. Reminds me of my dad."

"If that's the case, I'm guessing you got your looks from your mom."

Danielle smiles and I can see the hint of a blush. "I meant we used to go fishing when I was a kid."

"Yeah well, just—"

"Dom look!" The awe in Danielle's voice can only mean one thing: she's spotted the crabs.

I look up, prepared to follow Danielle's gaze to the bridge, but instead she's begun walking toward the edge of the pier, pointing out toward the river with her mouth wide, her eyes unblinking.

"Look at all the boats."

I hadn't noticed them from the bridge—the wall had blocked not only the assembly of crabs, but also the view of the river wide. But I can see them now, dozens of boats, from catamarans to luxury yachts, their shapes fighting through the low fog and white backdrop of the atmosphere, adrift on the water.

It all makes sense, of course. The day the snows came was a beautiful Sunday in May, which would have meant the boaters of this and every other waterfront community would have been out on the water, starting early in the morning and soaking up the day with fishing expeditions and drinking jaunts, not wasting a single moment so as to justify their hefty investments. Most of the boats weren't docked at their piers right now because they were all stranded on the water, unmanned.

"Do you think...I mean the sailors...that they all..." Danielle cuts herself off.

"I don't know about all, but I would think it safe to assume at least some. Let's just try to see if we can get this thing started."

I pull out the choke and shift the throttle to the start position, and then I pull the starter rope once, slowly, and then a few more times until I feel the resistance from the starter. "I think it's going to turn over," I say, hoping to attract good fortune with my words.

Danielle's eyes are wide with suspense as she nods, spurring me to give the rope another tug.

I pull the rope again, with force this time, and the motor spits for a moment, almost catching, before sputtering dead.

"This is the one," she says.

It's my turn to nod this time, and I take a giant breath before yanking the rope towards me with the full strength of my thighs and shoulders. The motor comes to life again and then retreats, but this time, just as it begins to die, it catches, barely, and then crescendos into a full growl.

"Yes!"

I push in the choke and turn the throttle to the 'Run' position, and then Danielle and I both stand in unison and begin waving our arms over our heads in the direction of Tom and Stella, signaling both our success with the boat and the urgency of the moment.

Stella points to the truck—indicating she'll need to get James first—and then she gives a thumbs up.

Danielle and I drop our arms, and I can't help but smile as I stare at the outboard motor, watching the propeller spin furiously above the water, fighting the rope line tying it to the pier. It's a small win, and one that's only momentary, since the boat may end up putting us in a worse spot than we are currently. But for now, I'll take it.

Danielle sighs and I can see that she is also looking at the boat, but the expression on her face lacks any levity. She looks up slowly and across to the bank on the opposite side of the river. "What if nothing has changed over there?" she asks, and then looks back to me. "And I don't mean immediately on that side—I can see the snow from here—but, like, anywhere over there."

I look to the spot where Danielle was just staring, understanding the question she's really asking is: *What do we do if the world is over?* I don't have the answer to that question, so I answer the one she asked. "Then we'll keep going. Eventually we'll cross into a town that isn't affected. It's a big world. We'll find it."

Danielle smiles weakly at this, and I'm relieved that she's accepted the answer, even if only to be kind.

I look to the place where Stella and Tom were just standing, but they're now out of sight, presumably having walked back from the bridge to take a route not as severely sloped as the one Danielle and I took to get down to the water. This extra delay has me slightly worried, particularly about fuel, since I have no idea how much gas is in the motor currently, and now that I've gotten it started, I don't want to risk adding more and conking the engine.

But my concerns about the delay are assuaged when our three companions arrive moments later, with James beside them, he, it would seem, having licked his wounds from our earlier discussion. He and Stella are smiling wide and laughing.

"Well done, guys," Stella says. "It's not my style exactly, but it's running."

Tom looks at the boat suspiciously, "So we're going with this one, huh?"

I raise my eyebrows and shrug. "I think we're lucky it started. So yeah, that would be my recommendation."

"You don't think we should take a look in any of the others? Just to make sure?" Tom's question isn't loaded; just a straight-shooting inquiry.

"I know how to work this one, but if you feel comfortable with one of those—"

"Oh Jesus! Oh my jumping Jesus!"

It's James, and my misjudgement about the source of Danielle's exclamation earlier is now, I assume, applicable to him. He's looking up in terror at the crabs on the bridge, except now they're no longer a couple dozen in number. They extend from one end of the span to the other, hundreds of demons perched upon the railing in a straight line of white, so uniform and compact that they're almost unnoticeable, having assembled into what could easily be mistaken as some ghastly architectural design.

Stella follows James' eyes and gags, a reaction similar to the one I sustained earlier, though hers is a bit more dramatic as she leans over the water and dry heaves.

Danielle has her hand across her mouth, staring in disbelief at the scene above us, and then, as if a thought suddenly popped into her head, looks over at me. She seems to notice my lack of an appropriate reaction. "You already saw them didn't you? You saw them and you didn't say anything."

I nod my confession. "I saw them earlier, when we were coming down the hill. But there were only a dozen or so of them then."

"There's gotta be hundreds now," Tom says, his voice distant and awed, so different from the typical Tom cadence. "You can't even count 'em there's so many."

"Let's go," I say. "This doesn't change anything. They're just watching us. Like they always do. I think if we stay away from them, keep a wide berth, then...I don't know." And I don't know; it's the beginning statement of wishful thinking. "Let's just go."

"Why are there so many?" James asks, still frozen in posture. "Where did all of the people come from?"

"They're not people," Stella replies.

"I mean the people who turned into those things after the snow. Where did they all come from? And why are there so many of them on the bridge?"

"I don't know, James," I say, now ushering the first of my passengers—Tom—into the boat. "There's lots of people in the world. But we should get going. If there are any of those things in the immediate area, on this side of the bridge, we're going to be fish in a barrel."

"But there's so many *more* of them now. Remember back when it first happened? There weren't this many then. I was out in the snows for two weeks after the blast, alone, hiding in houses and stores, and even then I only saw them every few days. Now they're everywhere. They were all along the road the entire drive here. And, Jesus Christ, there's a thousand on the bridge. Are you telling me all of these people were out on the bridge when the snow fell? That doesn't even make sense."

There's a telling silence that permeates the group, and no one dares attempt an answer to the question, mainly for fear that we'll discover one doesn't exist. But I think it's to do with the melting snow. I think these crabs have always existed, and now, with the rising temperatures, they're coming out more often.

"James," I say, "we can explore these and other questions later. Now we have to go."

Danielle and Stella quickly board the boat, and I step in behind them, eager to get away from this pier and on our way to search for the world that left us.

James never takes his eyes from the bridge, but he finally begins to back his way toward the edge of the pier and the boat, and Tom has to jump up and grab him at the waist just a step before he collapses into the freezing water. James is stunned back to the moment and quickly finds his senses and his seat in the boat, though his stare immediately returns to the perched crabs.

With everyone now aboard, I unmoor the craft and shift the motor up slowly, making a smooth departure from the pier. Within seconds, I'm steering the small boat across the river towards the far shore.

The eyes of my passengers are still riveted on the bridge, which now towers above us on the starboard side, but my attention is straight ahead, locked on the obstacle course of stray boats in our path, the fog shrouding some of them almost entirely.

Some of the vessels have been anchored and now bob listlessly on the waves, waiting patiently to resume the purpose for which they were made, to skid the waters at the command of their owners. But others are simply drifting freely with the current, desultory crafts of all sizes that have been abandoned by their captains and now search hopelessly for a new master. There's no telling from how far away the skeleton ships have come—it's been months now since the blast—and my imagination takes over, envisioning the world at large. What must the oceans and seas across the globe look like if the event has indeed affected the entire planet? The image is unfathomable, too big to think about right now, and I force myself to turn back to the issue immediately in front of me.

I continue at a steady pace, keeping as wide a berth as possible from the other vessels, but the further into the river we get, the more the boats litter the route, and I'm now forced to turn east toward the bridge to avoid smashing into one of the unseen strays. I think I can see most of them clearly, but there is just enough of a film of fog that I'm petrified about steering us into one of the smaller vessels or buried anchor lines.

East, however, is the direction of the bridge, and though the path of ships is clearer this way, we're now heading directly towards the crabs. We're still far enough out that I don't think we're in any danger from them, particularly not with them almost sixty feet above of us. But they continue to stare at us, still virtually motionless, and though I don't think they'll jump from the height of the bridge, I have no experience on which to base that theory.

I finally ease the boat into a nice gap that has formed between the bridge and the flotsam of boats, and as far as I can see, the route is clear from here all the way to the northeast bank of the river. Straight ahead on this trajectory should bring us to our destination in only minutes.

But before I can lock my brain in fully to my destination, a large cruiser yacht suddenly appears in my periphery. It seems to materialize from nowhere, just off to my left, and it sways my full attention towards it. I'm not sure what it is about the boat that intrigues me—other than its size—forty feet, at least—as well as the fact that it was so hidden by the fog and now looms large above the water. It looks brand new, beautiful, and it's anchored just close enough to us that I feel almost compelled not to pass it by without investigating. It floats isolated at just the right distance from the other anchored boats that it feels almost like it's calling to me.

I nudge the tiller towards me slightly and begin to head in the direction of the cruiser, while still keeping a general line on the course of the far bank. If we simply remain on our current progression from this point on the river—about a third of the way across—we should reach the far shore in a matter of minutes.

But the draw of the yacht is too strong, and I pull the motor towards me further and give the handle a gentle twist. Our boat is now headed directly toward the cruiser.

"What's the plan here?" Tom asks, noticing our course change. He's the first to finally turn his attention away from the bridge,

I get the sense that Tom will detect any bullshit from me, so I keep it honest. "I just want to see what went on here. I mean, look at the size of this thing. I feel like there could be something useful in there."

In seconds, I'm slowing up beside the cruiser. I have no immediate sights on boarding it, not without a solid assessment of the danger first, but I would like to get at least a superficial look at the craft.

Tom squints and looks up toward the cruiser, and then turns back to me. "Did you see any movement or anything?"

I shake my head and then crane my neck upward, trying to get a glimpse into the cabin. I don't know what I'm looking for exactly, other than an obvious indicator that the crabs are on board, some type of motion or sound perhaps. From this vantage point, however, although I can't see much, it looks pretty quiet inside.

Tom looks back to the cruiser for another evaluation. "Not sure about this, Dom. I'd say there's a good chance at least one of those things is on there. You believe that, right?"

I nod. "Of course. I just wanted to get close enough to see if we could get any kind of feel for what's in there. Because if it is abandoned—if we can determine that for sure—well, I would think a boat this size could be stocked with some pretty good stuff. A gun maybe. Food for sure."

Tom nods and raises an eyebrow, accepting the possibility.

"And there could also be survivors, I think that's a possibility too, people who avoided the first snows and then decided to stay out on the water. Maybe they saw the turning of some people on the bridge and then decided to keep away from the shores until...I don't know. The coast was clear?"

"Or maybe they came out after," Danielle adds, now also focused on the boat. Stella and James' attention have also turned in its direction. "They could have fled the shores and decided to hold up out here until things normalized and the weather turned. And if that's the case, like Dom said, they probably would have tried to bring as many supplies as they could carry with them."

I hadn't even considered the notion that Danielle has just raised. Maybe some of the boaters didn't get stranded on the water during a pleasant Sunday outing; maybe some of them made an *escape* onto the water after the snows fell and they heard what had happened. The early broadcasts of the event suggested the incident might have occurred everywhere, and though doubt about the validity of those radio reports now rage inside all of us, I decide fleeing to the river is probably not a good sign. That would suggest—to me at least—a general lack of safety on land, which means that any refuge from this madness is farther than the just the northern shores of the Maripo River.

But these thoughts are a combination of speculation and my own mind's fear-mongering; I don't know any of this to be true. I force myself to hone my focus back on the matter at hand.

I stand on my tiptoes to try to see through the tempered glass of the side window, but I'm too low and the glass is too dark. The increased possibility that there are survivors on board, however, has altered my apprehension about exploring the vessel. At this point, I fully intend to have a look inside.

"Danielle makes a good point," I say. "I think if we don't see any signs of those things in the next few minutes, I should board. I think we need to take a look."

James looks at me for a beat and then scans the faces of the group one at a time before returning his gaze to me, a look of confusion now evident. "Isn't that what we're doing? Aren't we taking a look right now? What's the point of boarding?"

"I just told you, James, there could be supplies."

"I thought you were in a hurry to get across the river. This was your idea. Stealing a boat and heading to the opposite side of the river. And now that we're on the way, halfway there, you want to start pillaging abandoned ships like Lewis and Clark."

The professor in me wants to explain to James that Lewis and Clark weren't pirates, but I resist the urge, knowing these corrections would only be counterproductive. "I *am* anxious to cross, and we will, but we're here now, and if there are supplies on this boat—or survivors—we can't just bypass them. Besides, if we can get *this* boat started," I shrug my eyebrows and tilt my head toward the cruiser, "wouldn't you rather be on this thing?"

"If there were survivors, they would have come out by now? And I don't really care about going cruising another three minutes in luxury. I just want to get there and find some place that isn't covered in snow."

James is still a kid, eighteen or nineteen if I had to guess, so I give him some space to emit his fear. But my patience is starting to wear thin with him. He's allowed to be afraid, but he's getting a little too loud and panicky for such a precarious setting as a rinky-dink motor boat on an icy river.

"I understand, James? I'm just saying this boat would be a nice option to have if we decided we needed to stay out on the water for a time. And though you're probably right about the chances that there are no survivors on board, there is a possibility. This boat has living quarters inside it. There could be people sleeping below deck. Or hiding."

Hiding.

My mind suddenly fills with the memory of our escape from the mad colonel back on the exit ramp. It was a surreal scene, he and his soldiers emerging seemingly from nowhere, appearing on the road like some deranged military oasis, a beast of metal artillery at their backs, one that was subsequently turned loose in an attack that was nothing less than an attempt to blow us off the planet.

The colonel—and, presumably, some other government entities whom we've yet to meet—had engaged in some kind of devil's pact with Stella's business partner, Terry, with the intention of carrying out their demented experiment of bombs and snow and crabs at any cost. I fear now if these organizations are willing to employ a tank to patrol the grounds of College Valley, it isn't unthinkable that some type of comparable vessel was currently patroling the Maripo River. Suddenly I begin to feel very agoraphobic.

"But I'll leave it up to the group," I say, now hedging a bit. "If this seems like a less than brilliant idea, too dangerous, I mean, then we'll keep going."

I can see Tom give a slight nod, almost a reflex of affirmation to the idea, with James seeming to concur by taking a deep breath, thankful I'd come to my senses.

"Well, shit, Dom," Stella says, shaking her head in frustration, "you had me convinced ten seconds ago that we should loot this beauty, and now you want to scrap your own plan?"

"It was never a plan, and I didn't say I wanted to scrap it. I'm just willing to take a vote."

Danielle speaks up, filling in my indecisiveness with a calm resolution. "I think your first instinct was the correct one,

Dom. I think we should investigate. We're going to need supplies at some point, and there's no guarantee they'll be anything waiting for us on the other side."

"Well if there's nothing waiting for us on the other side, then we're dead anyway," James whines. "So what difference is a few cans of tuna going to make?"

"I'm actually more interested in the possibility of weapons. We have one shotgun, and we're down to our last box of shells. We need to start stocking up on things other than food. There could be medicine, fuel, flares, a dozen other things we could use. In fact, if you ask me, I think we should make the rounds through all of these boats and get as much as we can."

"Are you kidding?" James is flabbergasted, and I can see the tears forming in his eyes as he throws up his hands.

"So let's take the vote. Like Dom said. Everyone who thinks we should give it another minute and then board the...what is the name of this thing?"

Danielle cranes her neck toward the bow, struggling to read the two-word moniker painted in fancy gold script along the hull.

"The *Answered Prayer*," Danielle chuckles. "Just in case anyone was conflicted in their decision." She raises her hand, casting the first vote to board.

My hand goes up second, followed by Stella's. We give a couple more beats to allow either Tom or James to join, but they abstain. Their votes don't matter though, we have a majority.

"Great," James says, calmly this time, resigned to his fate. Tom remains pragmatic, unmoved by the result.

"Boarding wins by a nose," Danielle announces.

I feel it's time to exert my leadership role again, and I quickly declare, "It's going to be me though. Alone. That was the deal."

Danielle frowns and raises her eyebrows. "First off, I never made any deal. Second, why would you be the one to go? Because it was your idea? Sorry, it was your idea to go in that house alone, and if it hadn't been for me, your bones would still be there getting picked over by buzzards."

"That's a bit of a low blow, but one I'm willing to forget about this time."

Danielle shrugs, and a tense silence fills the boat.

"So then it should be you that goes alone?" I ask finally.

Danielle nods confidently, as if the answer is obvious. "It should."

I feel the rest of the group staring at me, as if this moment is a decisive one in determining the leadership dynamic for the rest of our time together. I consider, however, that perhaps it's not the group who is judging the moment in these terms, only I.

"Well, you've proven you're a good shot, and we've only the one gun, so I'll stand down. If everyone else is comfortable with you going, then I am too."

I search the faces of the group for tacit responses, and Stella and Tom give me soft nods of approval. James just shrugs and looks away, rolling his eyes, a signal that his views aren't considered anyway, so what difference does it make what he thinks?

I push the lever forward and guide the motor boat in a circle until we're now parked perpendicular to the cruiser's stern. At this point, Danielle can step easily onto the low swim deck of the *Answered Prayer*, and within seconds, she's on the mysterious craft, shotgun in hand, moving toward the front of the boat.

And then we hear the first splash.

The sound explodes in my ear with no less force than the blast that started this whole story. I can't immediately tell from which direction it's come, but I have my suspicions.

"What the hell was that?" James asks.

I turn to look up at the bridge and the line of roosting crabs, and at first glance, the formation looks unchanged, an immobile grouping of alabaster statues. But as I scan farther down the line, toward the far end of the bridge, I can see the first gap of light shining through. I follow the sight line down from the railing to the water just below it, and I can see the ripples flowering out and then dissipating.

"Look!" Stella whispers, pointing back towards the railing.

I follow her finger and can see one of the crabs standing straight up now, tall and stiff like a bowling pin, its feet still appearing to be wedged between the railing and the barrier. It stands that way for a beat, and then, with no signal at all, it topples forward, tumbling over the side of the bridge as if it had been shot from the back. Two more crabs rise in the area of the previous one, perhaps two or three crabs down, and each fall into the water as casually as if they were preparing to lie down on a mattress. Two more follow over the side, then two more, all collapsing from the same general vicinity into the Maripo River. This continues for several minutes, as more crabs fill in the empty spaces left by the jumpers, and then jump themselves. Four, five at a time, nonchalantly, until dozens have gone over the side.

The gruesome sounds of the crashing bodies makes me cringe, their flesh splashing and slapping violently as they land. But I can't look away, and within seconds, the river directly below the bridge becomes a battlefield of white, the crabs hitting the water and one another like mortar fire.

At first, there's not much movement from the creatures once they enter the water, and many appear not to have survived the impact. Most disappear for a few seconds and then bob to the surface for a moment, and then ultimately sink beneath it again. Others lie listlessly atop those crabs that have survived and which are attempting to tread water, flailing their arms desperately, searching for the skill to swim.

But then the activity in the water begins to increase, and it seems that the impact has only stunned those I thought dead. Almost all of them seem to have survived the fall now, and those that had sunk beneath the water a second time have resurfaced, desperate to keep their heads above water.

They learn quickly, and now there are dozens of crabs, floating together in an island of albino flesh. The stragglers who missed the mark from the bridge and are on the outskirts of the island drift in to join the huddle, and the floating mass of crabs waits patiently until those that form it have collected all of their viable mates.

I have to assume that it is we on the boat who have precipitated this bizarre display from the crabs, but at first they don't appear to be making any effort to swim towards us.

But they continue to tighten their huddle, patiently waiting for those who haven't quite mastered the treading technique to do so. There are at least seventy-five of them now, perhaps a hundred, and the sight of the white bodies on the black water conjures thoughts of cancer.

And then it begins to spread.

The white splotch suddenly starts to change, extending from a circular blob to one more elongated, forming into something resembling an éclair. The mass continues to stretch in this way, growing longer and thinner, and, after several minutes, has a true design. It's a bridge, an extended span of bodies about four crabs wide.

And, of course, the bridge is building in our direction.

"What are they doing?" Danielle calls from atop the cruiser, her attention aimed in the same direction as the rest of us.

"Hey," I snap, "you can't lose your focus." I'm as riveted as anyone by the beasts spanning out towards us, but I understand the potential for danger aboard the cruiser as well. "I don't know if we have a lot of time. I would go ahead and assume not. So stay on task and if there's treasure to be had easily, grab it. Otherwise, don't linger. Let's not push this anymore than we need to."

"Push what? What do you think they're...you think they're coming for us? No way. There aren't nearly enough of them."

"I really don't know, Danielle. But why tempt it?"

The fact is I do know what the crabs are doing. I saw the same type of behavior back at the college, immediately after I broke out the window with the Dutch oven in the student union. Maybe it was just the noise that had provoked them then, but it seemed to me, even at the time, they had recognized an opportunity. Before I could really process what I was seeing on the ground, the crabs had begun to build their bridge of bodies up the wall of the building and toward the new opening.

And it's what they're doing now, seizing an opportunity, working with that same group relentlessness—like ants—attacking with commitment, willing to sacrifice themselves without thought.

The white bridge of flesh extends rapidly, and now, after it has evidently been built to its proper specifications, four of the beasts that made up the structure are now atop it, traversing it like pedestrians, knuckle-walking like chimpanzees to the edge of the floating bridge. At that point, they plunge back into the water, connecting with each other in a line, forming the next piece of the expanse. It's a type of natural genius, no doubt, instinctively understanding the process, like a spider forming its web or a beaver its dam.

And I can see that the bridge makers are becoming increasingly at ease in the water—treading the river more effortlessly than before, perhaps rediscovering the skill from their past lives through some primal instinct or abominable undead evolution.

The bridge of bodies continues to narrow and tighten in formation, and slims from four bodies wide to three, and it's obvious to me that the crabs are learning. Not only how to tread water, but also the dimensions necessary to create a bridge that can reach our boat more quickly. Why waste an extra couple of bodies for the width of the bridge when they'd be better served lengthening it?

The crabs at the very back of the bridge, those who served as the first planks of its construction, continue to climb up and make their way to the front, but for the first time I realize they've stopped adding bodies to the whole of the bridge, apparently having all they need now to get to us.

I look back up to the remaining crabs on the bridge and see they've stopped falling, somehow seeming to understand that their troop numbers in the water below are now sufficient. There's no sense wasting resources.

"Are they coming toward us?" James asks, a comically obvious question as far as I'm concerned, but I realize the concept may be too outrageous to believe, particularly by someone who hasn't seen this behavior previously.

"It looks that way," I say, no longer watching the water, my attention now back on Danielle and the *Answered Prayer*.

"How can...?"

"Wait," Stella says from behind me. "Look. They're...stopping."

"I noticed. They're not falling from the bridge anymore."

"No, I mean they've stopped building." Stella sounds rapt, as if entranced by the behavior, like a mad scientist taken over by wonder at his creation.

I prepare to dispute Stella's claim, until I turn back to the river and see that she's right. They have stopped, about fifty yards away from us. The crabs in the water have settled into a steady tread, and the two beasts standing atop the fleshy bridge just stare at us, watching.

"Danielle, how we doing up there?" I call, keeping my eyes fixed on the river. "Danielle!" I repeat, louder this time, but still no reply.

I turn toward the cruiser and see that Danielle has vanished from sight.

"Shit! Danielle!"

"Danny," Tom calls, his face white with panic.

"She's alright."

"You can't know that, Dominic." Tom's voice is calm, always calm, but there is pain in his eyes, fear.

"I'm going aboard," I say, but as I make a move to board the cruiser, I hear a light splash, followed by another. I turn back to the water. "What was that?"

"They jumped in," James replies, stammering the words out past his fear. "The two on top, they just jumped in the water. Why would they do that?"

I stare at the water around the crab bridge for several seconds, waiting for the creatures to resurface, but there is no breach of the water. "I don't know, but keep an eye out. I'm going to look for Danielle."

I hop the narrow gap between the Sea Nymph and the *Answered Prayer*, and in seconds, I'm up the back of the boat and am standing in the cockpit scanning the view. "Danielle!" I call toward the bow.

"I'm down here."

The voice is muffled and has come from below me, and I look down to see a small hatch in the floor. I pull up the door of the hatch and follow a ladder down to a cabin where Danielle is standing, a pirate's smile on her face.

"Pretty sweet, am I right?"

I give the cabin a cursory glance and then nod. "It is. What did you find?" My voice is hurried, one eye on the hatch.

"There's not much food, unfortunately, but there's plenty of booze. Rum mostly—kind of cliché—but there's also a few bottles of wine, a bottle of—"

"What about any weapons," I interrupt.

"I haven't found any guns, but there is a set of filet knives that could come in handy."

"Did you find any keys?"

Danielle's eyes get wide and she smiles. "I didn't even think to look yet. Let's check the ignition."

"I did, they aren't in there."

"Then why did you ask?"

"I meant a spare set. Hidden somewhere."

"Is that common, to keep a spare set on board?"

"I have no idea, but if I owned a boat, I would keep a spare key somewhere. I mean, what if you sailed to Tahiti and then dropped your keys in the ocean. How the hell are you getting home?

Danielle shrugs. "Airplane?"

I ignore the smart-ass reply. "Maybe Tom has an idea where someone might keep a spare set. Anyway, the crabs in the river are starting to act strange—stranger than usual—I don't think it's going to be safe for us out there much longer."

"What are they doing?"

"I'm not sure, but those things are...I don't know if smart is the word exactly, but they're acting very organized. They seem to be in some type of holding pattern for the moment, but we need to get across this river. This may have been a bad idea."

"Okay, I'll take what I've got and go check on the group, you keep looking for keys. Though truthfully, I'd much rather stay on this beauty for a few hours longer. No offense, but that rickety old motor boat is a pretty big downgrade."

I frown. "You know that's not my boat, right?"

Danielle shrugs and then heads up the stairs to the main deck. She's carrying a satchel with a drawstring pulled tight,

inside is presumably the alcohol and fishing knives she referenced, and whatever else she failed to mention.

I stay below as ordered and continue searching the cabin,
opening several drawers and cabinets in the yacht's small kitch-
enette, including several pull-down, glove compartment-like
spaces that would be perfect for keeping a spare set of keys. I
have no luck, however, and I quickly turn to inspect a carved-
out sleeping area on the opposite side of the same room.

I walk a few steps over to the foot of a twin-sized Murphy
bed, looking for more compartments or drawers, but the bed-
room area is essentially just a bed in a corner, and there aren't
many practical places where someone could hide a key.

My search there ends quickly, and I turn my focus now to
two thin doors that sit closed at the back of the cabin. The first
door is of the sliding variety and looks to be a closet, but the
second one is knobbed, with a silver passage-door lever which
I assume opens into the cabin's bathroom. It's as good a place
as any to search, I decide, and as I move to press down on the
lever, a bumping sound penetrates the cabin wall from somewhere behind the door. I freeze for a moment and then slowly
pull my hand away, and then I stand still for several beats, waiting for the sound again.

I lean my cheek gently against the door now, placing my
ear just barely against the panelling, looking off to the side like
a doctor listening to a heartbeat. But I can't hear anything. I
put my hand on the knob again, and this time I push the handle down, releasing the latch. The door cracks just an inch, and
then I hear the screams.

They're coming from outside.

I inhale a gasp and my throat seizes the sound halfway in. It takes me a moment to place the sounds of the screams—my first thought is that one of the white monsters will come bursting out of the bathroom—but I eventually process the source of the cries and rush back up to the top cabin.

From the cockpit, I can see them. Two crabs are surfacing in the water only a few feet away from the boat. I assume they're the two that were atop the floating bridge and had entered the river just before I came aboard the *Answered Prayer*.

"Danielle!" I call instinctively.

Danielle is standing below me on the swim platform with the shotgun aimed at the water in front of the Sea Nymph, which is beginning to drift away from the yacht. It's still close enough to jump the gap, but it won't be for much longer.

"I've got them." Danielle says, a steely confidence in her voice.

"You can't have both of them," Stella says.

"Everybody needs to get off!" I yell.

"Did you find keys?" Tom calls up to me.

"No, but we'll figure it out. Just get—"

Danielle fires the first round into the water, but I can't see any result of the shot other than the explosive blast of water shooting straight into the sky. I wait for the air to clear, but I still see nothing.

I look out to the bridge of crabs in the distance, to judge their reaction to the firing, but they seem unfazed.

"Where did they go?" James asks no one in particular. "I can't see them anymore."

I lean over the railing of the cockpit and look as deeply into the water as my eyes will allow, but I can't see them either.

It is possible, I suppose, that Danielle hit one of them with the shot—which would explain why that one is no longer visible—but she certainly didn't hit both.

"You all need to get off," I repeat. "If you don't do it now you'll have to jump in and swim. At least there are plenty of towels and clothes on board if that's your choice."

"Swim?" Stella questions.

"Or get off right this second. I know what my decision would be."

Tom and Stella both heed my call and less than thirty seconds later they're both aboard the *Answered Prayer*, standing beside Danielle.

As before, however, James is lingering.

"James, let's go!" Stella calls. "What are you waiting for?"

He backs slowly from the front of the motor boat, keeping his eyes peeled for the swimmers, and then finally turns his attention to the stern and Danielle, Tom and Stella standing on the *Answered Prayer*. He hesitates though, noting the distance the boat has drifted from the yacht. "What? What happened?"

"Can you make it, James?" Tom asks, nodding as he does, imparting the power of suggestion.

"I don't want to miss. It's too far."

"Jump in and swim then. It's one second and then we'll pull you out."

"No way," James answers, leaving little doubt about his willingness to plunge into the icy Maripo River. "I'll just pull the boat closer."

I consider this actually the better decision, one I'd resisted earlier for fear of the motor noise drawing more of the crabs to us.

James makes his way to sit on the stern seat and fire up the Nymph, and as he grabs the tiller of the motor, something reaches up the side of the hull and over the gunwale, grabbing his hand.

I don't believe it at first, a trick of my eyes maybe, but now I can see that what has gripped him at the wrist is another hand, one very similar to his own, only much whiter. He tries to scream but the sound catches in his throat, and within seconds, he's over the side of the Sea Nymph and beneath the water.

"Get him!" Stella screams.

James' face bobs back above the surface, for just a moment, and it's the fear in his eyes that lets me know he's still alive. But it's only a matter of time.

"Danielle," I call down, my voice is calm but with urgency.

"I see him, Dominic. But if I hit James, that's not really going to help the situation."

I watch as Danielle adjusts her aim slightly, raising the shotgun first to her left and then to the right, up and then back down a hair, trying to calibrate every fraction of the impending shot, the anxiety that she may kill an innocent man hanging across her face.

But she can't pull the trigger, and soon James is back down beneath the surface. Danielle lowers the gun with a huff.

"Dammit," I whisper, and without another thought, I hop over the side of the cockpit wall and drop down, feet first, into the river. I can hear the calls to stop from Danielle and Tom as I fall—Stella, I assume, is in a state of shock—and the pleas continue as I rise to the surface, the frigid water pressing on my chest like concrete. I think again of my ill-fated reunion with

Sharon and the pleas from my companions for me not to enter my home.

I begin swimming towards the spot where I last saw James, and thoughts of my own death emerge for the first time since my meeting with my wife earlier in the day.

But drowning and freezing to death are only two of the possibilities; I also consider that an attack could occur at any moment by one of the two crabs, shark-like, exploding from the depths of the river and ripping me in half at the torso. I now expect such an attack, in fact.

But then some type of primal optimism buoys me, quite literally almost, and I remain hopeful that if Danielle took out the first of the diving crabs, and if the second one is still preoccupied trying to kill James, I should have an unmolested path to him. I have no idea what my plan will be if I actually find him, but that's a problem for future Dominic.

I break into a true swimmer's stroke now, alternating my breaths intermittently, turning my face to the icy water for two strokes, and then back out for two more. I move steadily like this for what feels like a mile, but must be ten yards or less, and then, as I'm looking off to the side during one of my breaths, I see it, the crab bridge that had been formed so uniformly and altruistically has broken apart. And the bodies that had created it are all swimming towards me.

I'm only a few yards from the Sea Nymph now—which gives me plenty of time to arrive and be out of the water before the horde of swimming crabs arrives—but my mission isn't to swim to the Sea Nymph, it's to save James.

I reach the boat and stop on the far side, grabbing the top edge for a desperate moment of rest. I can feel the early effects of hypothermia setting in now, and my coat now feels like an x-ray vest, the kind they lay across you at the dentist when they check for cavities. It's doing me more harm than good now, so I work it off me and lift it over the edge of the boat and drop it inside.

"Can you see him anywhere?" I ask breathlessly to the group, all of whom are standing on the swim platform, watching me with a mix of wonder and concern.

"Get out of there, Dominic," Danielle says softly, shaking her head. "They're coming."

"Do you see him!"

"No, but he's got to be...wait." Stella points to the front of the Nymph, and I turn to see that one of the crabs has James by the hair and is pulling him away from the boat, swimming with him in tow back towards the bridge.

It's a hopeless scenario for me; there is no way for me to catch up to him. "Shoot him!" I scream, not taking my eyes from the white abductor.

And with perhaps only a second's pause following my words, I hear the blast of the shotgun behind me.

A geyser of red water erupts into the air, followed by flying bits of white, wet flesh. I blink a droplet from my eyes, considering that perhaps the bead of water has clouded my vision and the prism has created the illusion of colors. But the color comes in clear now. It's blood. She did it. Danielle did it. She pulled off the impossible shot and saved James. At least for the moment.

The water spray and last bits of the crab's body splatter to the surface, and I look over at Danielle with what must appear to her like love in my eyes, though the feeling I'm experiencing is closer to awe. "You got him."

"I got one of them," Danielle replies soberly.

But that one shot was perfect, fatal, and within seconds James has surfaced, his nose barely breaching the water line. He looks scared and tired, but by all indications, he's okay, offering further proof of Danielle's acumen with the weapon. If her shot had hit James anywhere on his body, from the distance he is from the boat currently, he would be on his way down to the riverbed.

I swim ploddingly towards James, a flounder's stroke, no longer putting my face beneath the water, gasping for each breath the whole way. When I finally reach him, it takes every bit of my strength to grab him from behind, under the armpits, and pull him towards me. I make a few desperate, one-arm backstrokes towards the Sea Nymph, but I'm quickly fading.

Another blast from Danielle, and I know that one was to keep the horde of crabs at bay.

"Are you okay?" I ask James, my voice almost inaudible with exhaustion.

James nods. "I think so."

"Can you swim? To the yacht?"

He closes his eyes and nods again, stifling some deep emotion that, given the circumstances, would be out of place were he to release it now.

"Go then. I need you to do this, James. I can't carry you anymore or we'll both drown."

I release James and give him a last gentle shove forward, and then I follow in his wake a second later, watching his progress. For the first few seconds, it looks like he's going to give up and sink beneath the surface, but he catches his stride, and I can see a newfound hope in his stroke. He listens to my instructions and swims past the Sea Nymph and towards the cruiser.

I am almost completely spent now, freezing and tired, now in the full grip of hypothermia, and by the time I reach the Sea Nymph, I can't swim anymore. I look up and see that James has made it to the yacht and the group is pulling him aboard the *Answered Prayer.* Ah, the magic of youth, I think to myself, and I crack a tiny smile.

"Come on, Dom," I hear a female voice call, and at this point I can't tell if it's Danielle or Stella. It's a sign, perhaps, that I'm beginning to lose my faculties.

I can't swim to the yacht, I simply don't have the strength to make another stroke, but I have to find the power, somehow, to pull myself into the Sea Nymph. Simply freezing to death without trying is unacceptable.

I grip the gunwale with both hands and bob my body down three feet or so into the water and then pop back up, lifting my torso out of the water just enough that I can flop my upper body over the side. I grip my pants with my right hand and pull my right leg up to the gunwale, catching the edge of the hull with the top of my foot, barely hooking the toe of my shoe on the inside of the hull. I'm now straddling the gunwale, my left leg still hanging over the side of the hull, and with a final scream, I pull my body up and flop my left leg over. I'm now lying flat on my back at the bottom of the boat.

"Dominic, they're coming!"

The words sound like they've come from inside of a dream, but I recognize the voices and it brings me back to the moment.

They're coming.

I force myself to sit up, the icy water dripping from my hair and shoulders, puddling around me in the bottom of the boat. I'm shivering so badly now that I can barely keep my balance, even when sitting. The water that saturates my clothes is smothering, choking the breath from my lungs, but I fight the sensation, and, in spite of myself, knowing what I'm likely to see when I open my eyes, I turn back toward the horde that I assume is still approaching.

Before I look, however, I note from somewhere deep in my mind that there haven't been any more gunshots, and I take this as a good sign. But it could just mean they've dived too deep, yet another indicator that they're learning on the fly, that they're acquiring the skills necessary to survive in this new world that they now govern.

Or maybe Danielle is just out of shots.

I open my eyes and scan the water for the oncoming gang of white crabs, but now I can't see even one. "Where are they?" I whisper, hoping to convey the question to the group on the *Answered Prayer,* a group that is steadily drifting away from me. I try again, louder this time, but my teeth are chattering to the point that I can't hold my mouth open long enough to form a word.

"Dom!"

The call of my name sounds distant, and I look up to see that the idling Sea Nymph has now drifted at least thirty yards away from the cruiser. But the crabs are still nowhere to be seen, and I recognize that perhaps a window of opportunity has opened for me. Without another thought, I crawl over to the outboard motor and climb up to the stern seat. I'm so cold that

I can't bring my right hand to the throttle, so I use my left hand to guide it there, finally landing my fingers on the thick handle. I push the throttle forward slightly and the boat starts to move forward, away from the cruiser.

I grab the tiller and swing the boat out a few yards and then start to turn it, steering the boat back towards the cruiser, my shivering so bad that I have to readjust the course by the second.

But I get into a groove and I'm headed toward the yacht now, slowly, fearing that my lack of control with the steering might lead me directly into the yacht's hull. Only ten yards or so now from the cruiser, I throttle back and let the boat's momentum drift me towards the yacht.

And then they appear.

I first see the dome of a bald white head rising from beneath the water, followed by the thing's shoulders and chest. And then a face appears, breaching the surface like some marine humanoid, corpse-like in its appearance, with only its eyes showing signs of life. Wet, blinking orbs of black.

Three more crabs follow, appearing beside the first on both sides, then a dozen more, and soon there is a procession of crabs lined up almost shoulder to shoulder, treading water, dividing the river between the Sea Nymph and the *Answered Prayer*. There have to be thirty bodies separating us. Maybe more.

I look up desperately to my companions who are all still standing on the swim platform, staring at the water, mesmerized by the scene of division below them.

"Jesus, God," James says.

The crabs are all facing in my direction, with their backs to the cruiser, but there's no guarantee they won't be turning to them soon. "Gggggett....uuuupstairs," I say, closing my eyes and motioning with my head for the group to flee to the upper deck of the boat.

"How are you going to get on?" Danielle asks. There is despair in her voice.

I shake my head. "I...I'll bbbeee fine. Just fffffind the kkkeys and..." I take a deep breath and steady my thoughts and my voice. "They're fffocused on mme now. I don't know why, bb-but it's a good thing. I'll lllead them away from here."

The boat has continued to drift forward and I'm now only about ten feet from the cruiser, with the crabs maybe five feet from me. Another minute or two and they'll be able to grab the gunwale and board the boat. I have to go now.

"Wait," Tom says, and I see him rush from the swim platform and up the stairs toward the cockpit. In what couldn't have been more than twenty seconds, he returns with a large plastic bag, sealed flat, about the size of a pizza box. "Catch."

Tom grabs the corner of the bag and flings it like an Olympic hammer thrower across the span of water. The bag clips the front nose of the Sea Nymph and tumbles inside. I look down and see that it's a vacuum-sealed package of what appears to be towels and blankets.

"You gotta strip down, Dom. Get outta them clothes. Pants too. You're gonna freeze to death if you don't get dry. There should be a spare jacket in there, but you're gonna have to dry out them pants somehow before putting 'em back on."

I nod my thanks to Tom, and I feel like I want to cry. That toss has likely saved my life.

I unzip the bag immediately and take out a blanket, wrapping it around my shoulders. I'll strip naked later. I need this blanket now.

I sit back down on the seat and wrap the blanket tight, and then, knowing my time is up, I grab the tiller and turn the throttle just a hair, just enough to start it floating off in the opposite direction of the *Answered Prayer*.

I barely move the boat to start—I just want to make sure the crabs behind me follow, and as I turn back toward them, I can see that they've started their encroachment. I look up and catch the eyes of Tom, and then Danielle, and I nod solemnly.

I continue to lead the crabs slowly, making sure not to rush, knowing that once I'm far enough away from the cruiser, I'll speed off into the distance and leave these white bastards in the middle of the river to drown.

# Chapter 3

I reach the bank on the opposite side of the Maripo River Bridge, several miles east of where the *Answered Prayer* sits anchored, and I pull the Sea Nymph up beside a pier that juts out from a riverside seafood restaurant called the Clam Bake. It's one of the more notable restaurants in the area—known more for its atmosphere than its food—but today it looks like it was abandoned some time during the middle of the last century. A rope sits limply atop the pier and I grab it, using my other hand to steady the boat against one of the pilings. I tie the thin rope to the cleat hitch of the boat, creating a knot that I'm sure sends sailors rolling in their graves. But I have more pressing matters than Boy Scout knots, and the only thing I can think about now is getting dry. I can no longer feel my fingers. Or toes. Or any part of my body, really.

I crawl atop the pier with the effort of a dying soldier, collapsing onto the wooden planks in exhaustion. The blanket wrapped around my shoulders is now completely soaked, clinging to me like some desperate starfish, and certainly doing nothing other than weighing me down at this point.

My entire body is numb, and the thought of taking off my clothes and exposing myself to the elements further seems insane. But Tom was right, it's what I need to do. Some parts of my body may already be dead, irreparable, but I'll die for sure if I don't get dry soon.

And there isn't much time to waste. I led the crabs away from the group, but I have to get back to the yacht as quickly as possible. Unless they can find a spare set of keys, my friends (it's the first time I've thought of them this way) will have no way of getting off the water. They have enough shelter and supplies to keep warm for the time being, but that won't last forever, and there's no guarantee they're safe from the rest of the monsters still perched atop the bridge.

Thankfully, the crabs—the ones prohibiting me from boarding the yacht—fell for my pied piper routine and followed me for what must have been, by my calculations, at least a mile and a half. They eventually tired and began to lag behind, and then they stopped entirely before disappearing beneath the surface. I have no way of knowing for sure if they drowned—I suppose they could have swum under water and made their way to shore—but in any case, I feel confident my friends are safe from those particular beasts for now.

But there are so many others. I think of the bridge barrier and shudder at the image that appears in my mind, hundreds of crabs still watching down on the water below.

I force myself to stand and then stumble down the length of the pier, holding the wet blanket tight against my shoulders. At the base of the pier is a low, waist-high gate that leads onto a patio of tables where the al fresco dining took place at the Clam Bake, no doubt a festive scene only months ago.

Beyond the patio, I spot a single glass door that has been opened wide and propped in place by what appears to be a small potted palm, though the snow on the leaves makes it difficult to know for sure. I instantly interpret the open door as a positive sign, since anyone who may have turned while inside the restaurant almost certainly would have found his or her way out by now.

Despite this logic, I enter the Clam Bake cautiously, stopping just across the threshold, attempting to take in as much detail as I can from there. If there is danger inside, my hope is that I'll be able to detect it before it's too late.

Not seeing any immediate threats, I slide the palm all the way outside with my foot and let the door close. I walk to the first of the bar tables and unload the wet blanket from my shoulders, flopping it onto the flat, wooden surface like a sack of flour. I then begin to unpeel the rest of the wet clothes from my body, removing the top garments first—coat, sweater, a pair of shirts—slapping each soaked item onto a different tabletop. As I make my way through the layers of clothing, each item suddenly feels like it's suffocating me, and I have to fight the feelings of panic as the garments rise past my neck and resist their final removal above my head, sucking at my face before releasing me to the air.

After I remove my undershirt, which is just as soaked as the top-layer shirt, I sit on the edge of a chair and begin to take off the bottom section of clothes, beginning with my shoes and socks. I have not a single feeling in either foot, and I'm afraid to look at them once the socks are removed, fearing some type of black mass of flesh will be staring up at me. But they're only red, and I have hope that total frostbite hasn't occurred.

Next, with great effort, I remove my pants, and instantly I begin squeezing my bare thighs and calves, kneading them like dough, trying to get the blood flowing so I can feel my legs again.

Finally, I pull off my underwear and drape it across a chair back, and then I remember the water-tight package of towels still in the motor boat, as well as the remaining change of clothes also inside. I was so eager to get to shelter that I forgot to bring them in with me, and the thought of going back outside is suddenly overwhelming. I sit naked on the chair, panic setting in, staring at the back door of the Clam Bake like it leads through to the gates of Hell.

I have to relax. Get dry. Look for supplies. Once I've done those things, my mind will settle and I can get back on the water. I can't collapse now, I have people depending on me, people for whom I now feel responsible. It was my idea to investigate the yacht in the first place. If we had simply gone across the river as planned, the crabs would never have gotten close enough to put us in the position where we are currently.

I decide to go back to the boat for the towels, and I slip my frozen feet back into my shoes about halfway, with my heels uncovered, squishing the back of my shoes down, wearing them this way just to keep the bottoms of my feet from contacting the frozen ground of the patio. I take a deep breath and then head towards the rear door that I've just entered. As I reach my hand toward the push bar, I see a small, distressed piece of driftwood on the wall above me with the words "Gift Shop" printed on it. The sign is painted ocean blue and faded, the lettering crab-red and cracked, and below it, drawn in crayon directly on the wall, is a yellow arrow that points vaguely toward a corridor off to my left and behind me.

Still freezing, despite having found the shelter of the restaurant, I put my hand on the door to leave, but my body won't follow through with my thoughts of retrieving the bag from the boat. I may be able to achieve the same ends in the gift shop, it says, and I turn back from the door, unconsciously

deciding to investigate the front section of the Clam Bake instead.

I walk through the main dining room and enter the corridor, the floor of which rises precipitously toward the front
door of the restaurant. I take two steps up the ramp and I can
see the glow of daylight at the end of the corridor, coming in
through the windows of the restaurant's lobby like a beacon. I
follow the light like a wayward ship in a storm-filled night.

The narrow walls of the corridor are pure kitsch, lined with
starfish and netting, clamshells and sand dollars, and I can't
help but smile at a cartoon drawing of an indignant shellfish
with the line, "Oyster? I barely know her!" in a bubble cloud
above his head.

At the end of the corridor are the bathrooms, and as I pass
them, prepared to turn the corner to the front entrance of the
restaurant, a loud, metallic noise bangs through the air, shattering the silence like glass.

I stop in my tracks, eyes wide, listening.

The sound again, followed by three more. *Clang! Clang!
Clang!* like someone striking an aluminium bat against a rusty
backstop.

I hold my breath. I can't see the source of the noise yet, but
it's close, right around the corner by the sound of it.

I take another small step forward, my toes now beyond the
border of the corridor, and from here I can see a small, convex mirror that's been positioned in the top right corner of the
front wall just below the ceiling. It's obviously some type of an-
ti-theft mirror, a way for the cashier or hostess to check on any
would-be shoplifters who might get a little frisky in the small
cove of the gift shop beside her. From my angle, I can barely

make out the shop itself, except to see that a folding security gate has been pulled down from the ceiling.

I look away from the mirror for a moment, searching the opposite side of the lobby, and as my eyes set on a large fish tank in the far corner, the clang of metal erupts again. I whip my head back to the right of the lobby and then up to the mirror, and I can see in it that the security gate is moving, vibrating. I stare at the convex glass without blinking now, waiting for it again, and then, in an instant, I see a body of white flash crazily into the reflection, slamming its body into the gate, the bars rattling again, somehow managing not to crumple.

One of them is locked inside.

Still naked, I walk into the lobby of the restaurant and stop first in front of the cashier station, lingering there as if I'm ready to pay my bill, studying the room for any weapon that I can grab in a pinch. I can sense the presence of the thing to my left, and then, out of the corner of my eye, it comes into view. The crab is nearly parallel with me, only a thin partition of gate separates us, and I can see its face pressed against the metal barrier, staring at me with large dark eyes.

I take a few steps to my left now, creating a wide berth away from the entrance of the gift shop as I do, and then I stop directly in front of the miniature store.

The shop looks like some type of mall store prison, and I can only stare in silence at the crab inside, which is now breathing heavily, standing hunched and pitiful like some emaciated bleached gorilla.

I almost laugh at the thought of a crab (one so very different than the kind they serve here!) imprisoned in the gift

shop of the Clam Bake, and I know there's a joke in there somewhere. Perhaps even one worthy of a spot on the corridor wall!

I'm mesmerized by the crab, which has the thrust of my attention, of course, but I can't help letting my eyes drift over the
stacks of clothes that hang from the racks and sit folded atop
the floor-to-ceiling shelves.

Pastel sweatshirts and sweatpants, thick and inviting, all
positioned just so, one of each type pinned against the back
wall as a display item, the words "Clam Bake" popping everywhere. The store also sells the more summery items like t-shirts
and beach towels, of course, and all of those have been crowded
onto a small table at the front of the shop, nearly touching the
security gate, resting obliviously only inches from where the
white crab is standing.

I'm naked and freezing; all of it looks like lobster and
caviar to me.

I hug my shoulders as I stare down the white monster in
front of me, and then I take a step forward. I'm still about six
feet back from the security cage, and the crab has no reaction
to my movement, continuing to look as docile as a pound pup-
py.

Another step—only a half-step really—and the crab remains still, expressionless but for the occasional blink of his giant black eyes.

And then I take one more step, a full step this time, and
that's when things change.

The single stride brings me to about three feet from the
crab and the metal barrier that divides us, and suddenly, as if
the step itself had toggled an On switch somewhere inside the
things body, its mouth snaps open and it hurls itself into the

cage. The motion is so quick it's as if the spring of a trap had been tripped, the mouth revealing a set of teeth that look designed for some human-sized piranha. The gape is primitive and animal, both in terms of width and contents.

I'm rapt by the sight, as I've not really witnessed one of the monsters up close in the throes of madness. I witnessed the mauling of Naia, but that was from a considerable distance, and the incident with Sharon was too personal for me to judge in the way that I'm doing now, undetached and objectively. The latter incident, which, unbelievably, occurred only hours earlier in the foyer of my own house, now seems more like a dream, one about which I've already forgotten most of the details.

The crab is raging now, but there is no growl or nonsensical, crazed words coming from it, only a low, choking hum, as if the sounds are caught somewhere low in its throat, like the loud buzz of cicadas on a hot summer's night.

I take a final step so that I'm now only inches from the crab, which has now begun again to slam its body against the cage uncontrollably, retreating a few steps and then catapulting itself back into the wide bars of the pen. The marks of metal are beginning to appear on its skin like brands, and wide, plum-colored gashes have begun to open in several places on its body.

I study the thing deeply now, cringing at every smash against the gate, its naked white body—aside from the new, self-inflicted injuries—so absent of definition or hair or flaw. It is in complete contrast to mine, with the unruly sprouts of hair popping wildly from my head to ankles, my genitals hanging limply like some useless appendage, a defect of evolution.

Another crash into the gate, and this time the crab sticks against it, its arms splayed like a beetle, its jaws latching onto to the metal latticework of the gate. I move my head a fraction closer, narrowing my gaze, and then I can see why there is only the sound of humming coming from it: it has no tongue.

The crab continues to stare at me, its eyes remaining expressionless, almost disinterested, a characteristic that only adds to the terror. There is no wrinkle of anger in the forehead, no slant of eyebrows (it has none) to convey its fury. There is only the relentless, shark-like motion of its jaws, a cold machine that has been programmed to feed. I can see from this distance that the crab's teeth aren't particularly large—they're human-sized even—but something about the angle in the gums looks altered, and the enamel of them seems to have been transformed, with each one having the definition of a tiny fang. An image of Naia appears in my mind again, and I can only imagine the terror and pain she must have felt.

The crab unlatches its teeth and peels itself away from the gate, and as I watch it hurl itself back again and again, the adrenaline of the moment is beginning to wear off. The cold of my body has returned with veracity, and I'm suddenly shaking almost uncontrollably now. The option still remains to return to the pier and get the rest of the towels and change of clothes from the motor boat, but the thought of going back out into the elements terrifies me, especially when I've got a treasure trove of warmth only a few feet away from me in the gift shop.

And an additional fear that the crab locked inside is somehow summoning his friends enters my mind from nowhere, and a sudden flood of claustrophobia overcomes me. It's impossible of course, this notion of murderous telepathy, but even if there's a fraction of a percent of possibility, I can't let it live. My goal now is to kill the crab inside the gift shop and retrieve the bounty within. And the trembling of my body lets me know that I need to do it soon.

I give the lobby another cursory glance, scanning it for a possible weapon, but I know what I'm looking for won't be in here. What I need—aside from the keys to the shop—is in the kitchen.

The keys. A weapon won't do me any good without a way in afterwards.

I walk behind the hostess station and cash register and reach into the waist-high opening beneath, rummaging my hands inside, searching. A notepad. A couple of pens. Some fabric that feels like an apron. I bend down to get a visual of the space, but I can't see anything other than what my hands have already felt.

I focus now on the cash register, an older type model with actual buttons instead of a computer screen, and I press the "No Sale" button on the right, not really expecting anything to happen. To my surprise, however, the drawer slides open with a ding, and I immediately feel around in the cash tray, flipping up the metal bill holders and fumbling under the cash for any sign of keys.

I remove the tray now and fondle inside the empty drawer, and, almost magically, my fingertips brush along the top of a small metal key. But as I remove it from its dark hiding place, I can see the key is far too small to be to the gate of the gift shop. It's for locking and unlocking the register—an activity, I consider, unlikely to be necessary ever again.

I'm shivering furiously now, and I start to reconsider my whole plan. What's the point of taking up arms and risking my life trying to kill the crab, if I have no way inside the gift shop?

And there's no question in my mind as to the soundness of the security gate; If the furious monster inside hasn't broken it down yet, it's not something I'll be able to open by force.

I'm standing hopelessly in front of the register now; my breathing is shallow and I'm finding it hard to concentrate. I assume these are signs of hypothermia, that my body temperature is getting dangerously low, and that within minutes I'll be completely delirious, curled up beneath the register dying. I have no choice—I have to go—and the thought of going outside again to retrieve the towels and clothes from the boat makes me want to cry.

My clothes from earlier are certainly still soaking, so there will be no relief from them in the elements, but I remember the apron beneath the hostess station. I pull it out and wrap the thin nylon smock across my shoulders. It feels like almost nothing, and it will be as useful against the winter as a chain link fence in a flood.

But it's something.

I pull the strings together beneath my chin and prepare to tie the apron in front of my neck in some pornographic Little Red Riding Hood way, and as I form the bow, something falls from the front pocket and lands on my toe, jangling to the floor.

"Ow!"

I look down and see them, a miracle of teeth and metal.

Keys. Three on a ring and regular-sized.

I stoop down carefully, not taking my eyes away from the floor, afraid that perhaps my mind has tricked me, created this jagged oasis beneath my feet to keep me inspired to go on. But it's no trick of the imagination; I can feel the cold bite of brass in the grip of my hand as I walk over to the gift shop gate, taking each step slowly to keep from falling over.

The crab has stopped its attacks on the gate for the moment, but it isn't far from the barricade. There is no way I can get close enough to test if the keys are to the gift shop—at least one of them anyway—but I know there has to be a match between the three of them.

Now on to the first part of the mission.

Inspired and replenished with a new burst of adrenaline, I turn back to the dining room, luxuriating in the feel of commercial carpeting on the soles of my feet. I don't linger though, and instead push through the double doors of the kitchen, lost in instinct now, keeping any premeditated thoughts as far away as I can.

The tile floor hits me like a gust of strong wind, but I keep on task, striding past the long metallic island, peering into the hollow spaces below as I go.

Not finding anything on the island that fits my needs, I move on to the dishwasher station, hoping to find something sharp and deadly there. But the cutlery rack has only forks and steak knives, not exactly the tools of a monster slayer.

I move to my left now to one of the food prep stations, which looks to have been unused, but as I move to the other side of the large, industrial range, I finally begin to see what I'm looking for. Strewn across the counters on this end of the kitchen are a variety of large knives, many of which appear to have been in the process of performing their business before suddenly being discarded by their handlers, presumably as they fled from the new white killers that were rampaging through the dining room.

The blades of the forged knives glisten in the light like stars, and I sift through a few of them before picking up two—a chef's knife and a cleaver. I press the blade of the chef's knife ever so gently to the tip of my index finger, and I can feel the strain of my skin to keep from splitting.

Armed now, I head out of the kitchen and back to the lobby, ready for battle.

I look straight ahead this time and walk directly to the gift shop, trying to stay focused, confident and composed despite my growing fear. I'm done with thinking though; it's time to act or die.

I can see that the crab has retreated from the front of the store now and is back towards the rack of clothes, crouched, ready to spring, staring at me with the same unconcerned look that they always seem to wear. I consider again trying one of the keys while the thing is backed away from the gate, but I decide instead just to go forward with this part of the plan. Once again, no more thinking.

I move as close to the gate as possible, my chest now brushing against the cold barrier, hoping to draw the thing towards me. It doesn't move though, and I realize that I'm too far away to trigger the instinctual reaction it showed earlier.

I kick the bottom of the gate and the crab flinches, cocking its head slightly down and to its left in the direction of the sound, like a dog listening to a question.

But still no move forward.

I begin to experience a new feeling of light-headedness now, dreamy and warm, and I assume it means that my body is starting to fail. I feel like I'm on the verge of delirium, preparing to die.

Desperate, I set the knives down on the floor beside me, nearly teetering over as I do, and then I rise back up and step a few paces backwards towards the front door of the restaurant. I close my eyes for a second, and then, with my mind as clear as Norwegian rain, I sprint full bore into the gift shop gate.

I scream as I slam into the metal, and though I've kept my arms folded in front of me to minimize the damage to my more delicate parts, the pain is immense, heightened by the cold of both the air and the gate itself.

The crab takes a step forward now, reaching the display table of sweatshirts before stopping. I don't know if it's the sound of the impact, or the mimicking of its actions that have stirred the imprisoned crab, or perhaps something else entirely. But I don't care; I just need it to come to me.

My heart is pounding with fear, but I will myself to stay pressed against the gate, hoping that the crab will get the scent of me—or the sound of my breathing or whatever it is that triggers it to madness—and will attack the gate as it did earlier.

I can see the thing is considering its next move, calculating, just like the ones on the bridge seemed to before jumping to the water and constructing their bridge. And now, based on this single crab's actions and the actions of his brood, I've come to the conclusion that these beasts do have control of their actions, but only to a point, literally, and once that point is crossed, the animal in them takes over.

The crab moves slightly to its right, its stare locked on me, and I follow it with my eyes, my body still pressed tightly against the cage, my penis and testicles feeling particularly vulnerable. But I hold my position.

Another step forward by the crab.

It's almost at the gate now and about three feet to my left, barely in the range of my periphery. It seems to understand that my judgement is thrown from this angle and my ability to avoid an attack impaired. If I wait much longer, it will be too close for me to pull away in time.

I take a final deep breath and then kick the bottom of the gate again, screaming this time, both from the pain on my foot and to enhance the disturbance. Almost instantly, not a full second later, from the corner of my eye, I can just make out the red flesh of the crab's inner cheek, opening its mouth to tear in to my face. Time to go.

I propel myself backwards just as the monster slams against the gate and presses its white skin at precisely the spot where I was standing a second earlier, only an inch of metal separating the two places.

The crab begins gnashing its teeth against the metal again, and I quickly stoop to the floor, in one motion sliding the two kitchen knives back toward me and picking them up, one in each hand.

I stand still for a moment, waiting for the thing to resume its routine from earlier, taking three steps backwards and then slamming into the gate. It takes a minute or two, but then it begins.

I let the first two attacks happen without action, getting the timing down.

Three steps back and charge. Three steps back and charge.

Once more, just to be sure.

And then I act.

On the crab's fourth retreat—three steps back—I lean my body forward, and then, going off timing alone, I rush the metal gate, mirroring the charge from the other side, the forged butcher's knife extended out in front of me like a bayonet.

I can feel the crisp resistance of bone and muscle envelop the blade, and the side of my grip presses against the cold crab's skin, sending a chill of a different kind through my body. From somewhere inside the monster there's the sensation of soft meat—a lung perhaps—getting skewered, and the coughing eruption from behind the gate seems to confirm it.

I pull away from the gate, and the feel of the blade sliding from the crab's body makes me gag.

But there's little time for weak stomachs, and I step away quickly, my eyes hula hoops, the blood of the crab coating the blade of the knife like caramel over a soft-dipped cone. The crab remains pinned to the gate, and there is no change of expression on its face. But the wound to its torso is significant, and the blood is gushing from it like a river.

It takes three steps back, more slowly this time, and rushes again, and I do the same.

This time I hold the knife higher, aiming it now, and as I slam against the gate, I watch the blade puncture into the chest of the crab, high on the left side, six inches or so beneath the shoulder blade.

The blood from this strike leaves no doubt that I've struck the heart, and with this stabbing, the crab collapses, grabbing the cage as it falls and managing to land on its knees.

The mutant human is gasping to breathe now, blood choking it on every inhalation. It's now on all fours, trying to keep its head up to keep me in its vision, but the energy is gone. It bows its head, blood dripping from its chest and mouth, the violent coughs beginning to sputter.

I set the chef's knife down and replace it with the cleaver. I grab the gate with my free hand and rattle it above the bowed head of the crab, and it follows the sound, looking up at me, its black eyes still showing no signs of anything but reptilian apathy.

But the strength of the thing is fading quickly, and it returns its gaze back to the floor beneath it, slowly coughing out the blood that continues to flood its mouth.

I swallow and close my eyes for a beat, and then I bring the cleaver down across the back of the bald white head below me. It's a clean strike, the large square blade catching the skull lengthwise, and without a sound, the crab falls forward into the gift shop gate and slides slowly to the floor. It twitches once, just barely, and then dies, its black eyes continuing to stare without an ounce of either fear or regret.

I toss the cleaver behind me and return to the hostess station for the keys, which I'd set on top of the register, hoping that would help me remember. I can barely recall my name now, or what I'm doing here, but I know the mission was to get inside the shop.

Within a minute of killing the crab, I've opened the gate and have begun to put on the first layer of Clam Bake novelty clothing. Another layer goes on. And then another. And then I begin to fill up shopping bags with all the towels and thick clothes that I can carry. But I need to move, to formulate my next steps, to figure out how I'm going to go about rescuing the people that saved me and that I led on the fateful journey across the Maripo River.

If they haven't found keys to the yacht by now, or found enough weaponry to keep the crabs at bay, then they're already dead. I have to try though. I have to return to the spot to make sure. And if they're gone, I'll figure out my next steps from there.

But for now, I can't move. For now, I can only sit on the floor of the Clam Bake gift shop, shivering, trying to hug the warmth into my bones.

# Chapter 4

I snap open the second of two large, black trash bags that I found beneath the bar and begin to fill it. The bags of clothes from the gift shop sit patiently by the back entrance of the Clam Bake, waiting for the impending adventure on the river. But I've also decided that, in addition to the clothes, stocking up on some of whatever is stored in the restaurant's walk-in refrigerator would be an even better idea, and the large, black trash bags an even better form of toting.

And the fridge renders quite the haul.

Containers of clams and oysters, tuna steaks and salmon filets, and enough ground beef to last a year, all taunt me from the tall racks of steel shelving. But it's all for naught. I've already made the decision to leave most of the good stuff behind in favor of less perishable items. Nearly-frozen loaves of bread and tortillas. Three boxes of croutons and a few cans of tomatoes. An industrial-sized container of Quaker Oats. I toss in a stack of cellophane-sealed rib eyes for good measure. Just in case.

With the second bag now filled to a comfortable carrying weight, I walk both bags out to the back door and place them next to the bags of clothes, and then return to the kitchen for one final assessment of supplies. On the way, I grab my open bottle of Heineken off the bar and take the final swig.

I step through the double kitchen doors and stop, scanning the kitchen a final time for anything light and useful. I set the empty beer bottle down on the steel counter, and as I do, I hear the sound of a man's voice.

"Check back there," one calls. "I'll check the kitchen. Somebody put all that stuff by the door."

Like a cockroach to an illuminated room, the man's voice propels me to scramble forward, grabbing the empty bottle of beer before I bolt, dodging past the kitchen island and barely opening the thick, sheet metal door of the walk-in refrigerator, just wide enough that I can squeeze in sideways.

There is no window on the refrigerator door, and it's almost certainly sound proof, so I put the empty bottle of Heineken on the floor at my feet and wedge it between the door and the jamb. I figure the bottle isn't likely to be noticed by anyone walking through the kitchen—at least not at first—and the gap will allow me to be able to hear if and when someone decides to enter. What I'll do at that point I haven't quite figured out—the chef's knife and cleaver are nowhere near, resting with the clothes and food on a table by the back entrance.

I can't see the man as he enters, but I hear the swinging flap of the kitchen door, followed by the low-pitched clicking of hard heels hitting tiled floor. The steps stop almost immediately, and I can picture the person perusing the room suspiciously, his eyes narrow, wary.

After a few more seconds, the footsteps finally resume, this time with purpose in the stride, confidence, and I suddenly think of the mysterious colonel from back on the exit ramp.

"What do you got, Jones?" I hear another man call. The voice sounds like it's coming from the dining area. "Anything?"

"Not yet," the heavy-footed kitchen-searcher answers, whose name I now know is Jones. "But I just walked in so give me a sec."

"You're not feasting on crab legs or something, are you Jones?"

"I'm feasting on your mother," Jones mutters to himself, and then calls, "Yep, you caught me, Abramowitz. Still looking for something to melt this butter though."

I turn back to the contents of the refrigerator, looking for anything that might be functional as a weapon, and I spot on the shelf, just to my left, a small, twelve-ounce can of chicken broth. I grab it, wrapping my fingers into a tight squeeze around the paper label, relishing the heft of the can. I return my gaze to the kitchen.

The gap created by the beer bottle that sits between the door and the jamb has given me a sliver of visibility, a narrow line of sight to the vicinity of the dishwasher's station. Jones finally enters my view and, instinctively, I take a step back, maintaining my vision of him. He takes another step and then stops, and I can now just see the backside of him on his right side, including his arm which hangs beside him, his hand gripping the butt end of what I can only assume is a rifle. From my vantage point, I can only see the top of the gun's butt, but if it isn't a rifle, it's a gun of some sort, and certainly one that's far more deadly than my twelve-ounce can of broth.

Jones takes another step toward the dishwashing station and is now out of my view, but judging by the sound of his boots, he's about to make his way around the kitchen island to start his journey back toward the doors that swing out to the dining room. It's a path that will take him past the refrigerator, and even if he doesn't notice that the door has been propped open, I can't imagine he won't want to check inside. I know I would.

"Holy shit!" someone calls in the distance, and I have no doubt the exclamation has come from the lobby.

The gift shop.

"Jones, get out here!" Abramowitz calls.

I hear the bang of the island as Jones makes his turn and rushes toward the kitchen doors, passing by the refrigerator and my watching eyeball by only inches as he flees.

Abramowitz's call has given me a chance, and, boldly, I push open the steel door of the refrigerator before I even hear the swing of the kitchen doors. I know Jones' focus is away from the kitchen now and on his partner, but I'll have little time to waste if I'm going to make it to my boat without being noticed.

I leave the trash bag of food on the floor of the walk-in, deciding that I will need all of my fluidity and stealth to flee the restaurant and reach the boat without being noticed. Besides, it's a two-trip effort to get the clothes and the food to the boat anyway, so even if I got the food to the door without a sound, I would need to leave it there anyway. Between the food and the clothes, I'm choosing the clothes for now. It may not be the wisest decision, I know, but I can't imagine feeling the earlier torture of the elements again. And I know the food is still in the refrigerator, so if the armed men don't take it with them when they leave, I can always come back for it later.

I step outside the kitchen doors and into the dining room, stopping at the bussing station on the opposite side of the bar, listening, trying to gauge where the men are currently.

There's only silence for the first few seconds, and then, "You think anyone's still here?" Abramowitz asks, a note of discovery in his voice.

"I'm not sure I even understand what happened here," Jones replies. "It certainly looks like this thing was killed though."

I can hear that the voices are coming from up the corridor, and though the men are speaking at a relatively normal volume, it sounds like they're standing right next to me. As the crow flies, they're probably fifteen feet away, and the partition between us offers almost no soundproofing. I have to stay quiet, but I can't wait much longer to get out of here. These men are intrigued by the crime scene for the moment, but they'll no doubt be moving on any moment.

"What's not to understand, Jones? You've seen what these things can do. I'm guessing this particular joker just mucked with the wrong guy on the wrong day. Some guy who probably didn't feel like being eaten today."

*I was just cold*, I think to myself, but if I was in the position of these men, I'm sure I would have drawn the same conclusion.

I move back to the rail of the bar and step lightly into the dining room, making sure not to veer into the view of the corridor. I then do a quick-walk beeline for the back door, my heels never touching the floor.

The large shopping bags of clothes sit like Christmas packages on the booth by the door, and as I pass the area, I pick the two bags up like a bandit and then back my way out to the patio in one motion.

The wind hits me like a bomb blast, but the air is nowhere near as cold as I had expected, even taking into account that I'm now wearing several heavy layers of cotton. It's warmer now, warmer even than it was a few hours ago.

I get my boat into focus and then walk, keeping my eyes straight ahead, fearing that if I look back to the door I'll somehow draw the men toward me with my mind.

I step past the last of the outdoor dining tables and off the cement patio, and then I push open the gate at the edge of the water that leads to the pier. I now have a direct path to my boat. But after just a few steps onto the weathered wooden planks, a wave of claustrophobia envelops me, and I nearly stumble off the side of the pier to the left. I know for sure I'm trapped at this point, with only freezing water and armed men around me until I reach the boat at the pier's edge.

But I reach the boat without incident and step inside it quickly, maneuvering to the back and the outboard motor. I find a relatively dry spot to set the plastic shopping bags, and then I stare at the lifeless motor, my heart in my throat as I prepare for the moment of truth.

I pull out the choke and pull the cord, and the motor roars to life like a race car, strong and ready.

And then, as if suddenly smothered by a blanket of clay, it dies.

"No," I whimper, my throat seizing.

I pull the cord again, but this time there is barely a sputter, the engine sounding now like someone in the final stages of tuberculosis.

"Hey!" a voice calls from somewhere to the left of the restaurant.

I'm not the least bit startled, understanding the eventuality of this moment, and I look up to see from the corner of my eye two men running around the side of the restaurant, coming from the front of the building.

"Stop!"

I pull the cord one last time, hopelessly, knowing that even if it starts I won't make it out of range of the rifles in time. And even if the soldiers decide not to go so far as to shoot me (and why wouldn't they?), they no doubt have a boat that can overtake me in seconds.

But the motor just wheezes anyway, keeping consistent with the metaphor of sickness.

There's a metallic click from the foot of the pier and then, "Put your hands on top of your head! Now! Now or you're dead in three seconds!"

I look up to see the faces of the two men, but they're concealed almost entirely by goggles and face wraps. Their dress looks military, tactical, but they don't match each other and one of the soldiers is at least six inches shorter than the other. I pause for a few seconds longer than the ultimatum time of three seconds, and then I lock my fingers across the back of my head, holding my chin high, never taking my gaze away from the men.

Within seconds, two more men, Jones and Abramowitz, I presume, exit the restaurant and are now running towards the pier. They stop next to the two other soldiers, and all four are now pointing rifles at me, staring down the sights.

"You can put the guns away, fellas," I say casually, "I don't even have a Swiss army knife."

"Why did you run?" one of the veiled soldiers barks. The voice is feminine, a woman, and she sounds a bit too nervous for my comfort level.

"*Because* I don't even have a Swiss army knife." I chuckle, trying to bring levity to the scene.

"Who's with you?" another asks. It's one of the men from inside the restaurant this time, and I know from the Midwest accent it's Jones.

"It was me who killed that one in the shop," I reply.

Jones pauses and lets his eyes examine me a moment. "That wasn't the question."

"I'm alone. There's no one with me. I was on the river, my clothes were soaked. I saw this place so I came in to get warm. And I noticed the sign for the gift shop. These bags—" I put the tips of my fingers through one of the straw, hooped handles at the top of one of the bags.

"Get your fucking hands back on your head!" the outside male soldier screams, mimicking the nervousness of his female partner.

I swallow once and begin to nod, my hands returning to the top of my head. "You're right. I'm sorry. I was just going to show you that I came here for clothes. I was freezing. All I have with me are clothes.

"Clothes didn't kill that ghost in the gift shop," Abramowitz says. "How'd you manage to do that with no weapon?"

The knives. I now realize those might have been a good thing to bring along, though in the position I am currently, they may have gotten me killed. "I did have a weapon inside—a couple of knives from the kitchen. But I don't have them anymore. I left them."

The four soldiers continue to stare at me for a couple of beats, and then the soldier who originally ordered me to freeze orders me to exit the boat and walk back towards them.

I come slowly, my hands still on my head, and as I walk past the group and towards the restaurant, I notice there is something a little different about these four. They certainly have the weaponry of soldiers, and the demeanor and movements as well, I suppose, but they're not dressed uniformly, and they lack some of the discipline and nomenclature of enlisted soldiers. From this proximity, they no longer invoke the images of the colonel who tried to murder me and my group back at the exit ramp.

My back is now to the soldiers, and one of them, I'm not sure which, taps the back of my head with the muzzle, encouraging me toward the door of the Clam Bake.

"Who are you?" I ask, knowing a question like this has the potential to be rewarded with the butt-end of the rifle finding its way to my skull.

"You don't fucking ask—" the woman starts—and I know it's her now who has me at the end of her gun—but she's cut off mid-threat.

"We're gonna hold off on the introductions on our end for a few more moments," Abramowitz explains. "Why don't you tell us who you are first. Once we're inside."

The woman leads me into the middle of the dining room to a table by the window, and then motions for me to take the seat next to the window that faces the bar. "This is lovely," I comment. "Did you reserve this?"

Abramowitz grins at the joke and then sits down at the seat facing me. The other three soldiers position themselves at various seats around the dining room, making sure that all entrances and exits are covered. "Now, let's get acquainted. Who are you and what do you know?"

"Name's Dominic. I'm an English professor. I know a lot about the Romantic poets. Coleridge. Byron. I know a bit about the Neo-classicists as well, but the thrust—"

"That's very funny, Dominic," Abramowitz interrupts, and then his grin wanes by half. "What do you know about this?" He motions toward the window, and the bleak landscape of the world outside. "How did you end up here?"

I have no reason to hold back on my story—at least not on the bulk of it—so I don't. I'm surrounded by four semi-automatic rifles, each of which has an index finger only millimeters from the trigger, and nothing I say now is going to make the situation worse. Besides, if these people wanted me dead, that deed would have been carried out by now.

I start with the first moments of the blast and the weeks at the campus with Naia. I include the details of my infidelity, not seeing any point in being discreet, especially since the events in my foyer with my wife are part of the tale. I tell them about my escape with Naia to the diner—and her subsequent death—and then our decision to leave, eventually ending up in my neighborhood where I discovered the thing that was formerly Sharon.

I omit the chapter about Stella and Terry's confession in the diner and their initial involvement in the experiment that led to this apparent apocalypse. And the part about Terry's connection with the colonel on the exit ramp also doesn't make its way in. These are large parts of the overall story, of course, but they're also chapters that, given the quasi-military appearances of the men and woman before me, could be connected to this particular group. My instinct is that they don't know much more about what happened than I do, but it could all just be an act to get me to spill everything.

"So we left Warren and headed north," I continue, "and drove until we got to the Maripo River Bridge. But as I guess you know, it's blocked." I look around the room now, studying the faces, trying to see if they actually do know that. I get only blank stares. "So that's when I came up with the plan to charter that lovely traitor of a boat right out there."

I point out to the pier and the dead Sea Nymph, and a wave of despair suddenly hits me like a right cross. Danielle. Tom. Stella and James. It's been hours now since I left them. If they weren't able to get the cruiser started, unless they found an armory of ammo on board, they wouldn't have been able to hold the crabs off for this long. And more ammo didn't seem likely. That boat was more of a pleasure cruiser, one for millionaire weekend guys; it wasn't made for the sort of guy who would be packing major firepower.

The image of my group suffering instills a renewed sense of urgency in me. "I got separated from my group. I had to leave them on the river. But they're expecting me to come back. I have to get to them. I have to help them." My voice is pleading, desperate.

"How did you get separated, Dominic?" It's Abramowitz again, his tone nonchalant, indifferent of my desperation.

"We...I...saw another boat, one I thought we could trade up to, I guess. Listen, we don't have much time. We need to go now. If you're still interested in my life story, I'll tell you the rest on the way, but I need to go after them."

"And how do you plan to do that?" the woman soldier asks. "Your boat ain't startin.' And even if it was," she scoffs and shakes her head, "if *I* was you, I wouldn't get in that thing if it was in a damn swimming pool."

"Wait. You mean you don't have a boat?"

She smirks and shakes her head.

"How did you..?" But I already know the answer. These soldiers haven't come from the Warren County side of the river. They didn't spot me from the water during some river patrol. They were already here.

"Got us a big ass RV though," she adds, and then smiles proudly at the laughing reaction of her partner.

I can hardly breathe now. The news that my river voyage has come to an end is debilitating, and a piece of me accepts that I'll never see my former group again. This doesn't mean they're dead, of course, not necessarily, not if they got the boat started. But I face the reality that this separation is bound to be permanent.

"We were hoping," I start, and my voice sounds distant in my ears. But I hold Abramowitz's stare tightly. "We thought that maybe, since they blocked the bridge off, that the blast and the aftermath had all been contained just to our side."

Abramowitz drops his eyes from mine. I look over to the aggressive male soldier and see that the residue of his smile, created by his female partner's joke—fades in a flash.

"How far does it go?" I ask him.

"Damned if we know for sure, bro," he says, his voice as defeated as mine. "We're not exactly getting the nightly news broadcasts over here either." He frowns and shakes his head slowly. "But we know where the edges of the cordon are. And we see them damn ghosts everywhere now."

Ghosts. It was the word James used back at the pier, and it's a more appropriate term in every way. The whiteness of them. The way they blend in silently with their surroundings. The fact that they've replaced their former bodies with a malevolent new force. Not like crabs at all. Except when they move.

"You all are soldiers, right?"

There's silence amongst them and then Jones speaks up. "That's right."

The heads of the other three soldiers snap up in unison towards Jones, their collective eyes nearly popping from their sockets.

Abramowitz seems to will Jones' eyes to his. "Don't speak again, Jones. You understand me?"

"Or what, Abramowitz? What are you going to do? Shoot me? Have me court martialed? What's the point of keeping secrets anymore?"

Abramowitz is seething now, and the two other soldiers seem ready to pounce if the command is given.

The thick coating of tension hovers in the dining room like poison gas, and I know if it comes to a head, it could be both Jones and me lying in a pool of our own blood on the carpet, a smoking bullet hole in the middle of our foreheads.

"I don't care what you know," I say pre-emptively. "I mean, that's not exactly true, I guess. I want to know what happened, of course, to the world, but first I need to get back to trying to save my friends. I put them in the danger they're in now, so it's my responsibility to get them out. I at least need to try. Please, just let me go so I can find another boat. What threat am I to you? Who am I going to tell?"

"Let's help him, Bram," Jones says, calmly now, the hint of pleading in his voice.

Abramowitz holds Jones' eyes until he drops them to the floor, shaking his head in disappointment. "That's not going to happen, professor. Even if my friend here is correct and the end of the world is at hand, we're sticking together until we find out what you know."

"I just told you everything I know. Which is apparently way less than you."

Abramowitz—Bram—pauses and then looks at his cohort, giving each member a full second or two, measuring them. "What Mr. Jones said is true. We are soldiers. We were brought in just before the event happened. None of us was ever told what was coming exactly or even what our mission was. Only that we were to guard the perimeter of a cordon and make occasional excursions into the interior. The day before the blast we were inside the cordoned off area, and each of us got separated from our troop at some point." He pauses. "We know now we were abandoned intentionally."

I note the nods from the other three soldiers.

"We met up with each other at one point or another and here we are. Stuck on the inside just like you." Abramowitz pauses and says, "Now that's my story. And I have a feeling what we heard from you was the abridged version of yours. I want to know more about your friends. Who they are exactly and where they came from. I get the suspicion there are a few gaps you left out in that first telling."

Abramowitz's story rings true, but I'm still reluctant to lay all of my cards on the table. "My *friends* are people I met at a diner a couple of weeks ago. I don't exactly know their deepest desires."

"No? Well I guess we'll see then." Bram stands and nods to the other two soldiers. "Smalley, Stanton, let's go." The two soldiers rise immediately and then aim their rifles back on me, motioning with their barrels for me to get up and follow Bram out the door.

"Okay, listen, maybe I do know a little bit more. But you have to promise me that if I tell you what I know, that you'll help me find my friends."

"Maybe we'll just hold your head over the sink and waterboard you until you tell us. There's always that option too." It's the outside male, whose name I now know is Stanton.

"Fuck off, Stanton," Jones says, apparently outranking the large soldier. "That's a deal, Dominic." Jones doesn't look at Abramowitz as he walks to the front of the restaurant.

Abramowitz follows Jones with his eyes and then begins walking behind him. "Okay, Dominic, I'll honor the deal. But first we're going to take a little ride.

# Chapter 5

The RV is, as Smalley referenced earlier, quite large, about the size of a small charter bus. But there is nothing military about it at all. Instead of the rugged camo look of an army truck, the vehicle looks like something picked off the lot of an interstate Camping World, the surprise gift of some rich dad who has impulsively decided to take his family on a cross-country summer road trip.

The RV can't be more than a year or two old, as the body of it still has that new, shiny factory luster; and the dark, swooshy, boomerang symbols that pop against the white sides and back of it give it the look of speed and transcendence.

Inside, the layout of the camper is nicer than most of the apartments I lived in for the first thirty years of my life. Leather couches and granite countertops line the interior, and there are at least two flat screen televisions anchored at the ceiling, along with various video game consoles below.

"You guys heading out to the Grand Canyon once the weather clears?" I ask from my seat at the elbow of two couches; Smalley and Stanton are flanking me on either side.

Abramowitz is standing at the threshold dividing the driver—who is Jones at the moment—from the living space where I sit currently. "You think your friends would appreciate the smart ass replies right now?" he asks. "Stranded out on that boat as they are?"

"Probably not," I concede. And then, "Well, maybe one of them would. So what do you want to know, Bram?"

Abramowitz scoffs at the familiar nickname and then retaliates with, "Everything you've got, Dom."

I stare the soldier down for a moment, trying to maintain some air of confidence, hoping to impart the seriousness of my character and the desperation of my plight despite my banter. "Everything I told you was true, but there is more. I know about an experiment." I pause, "Let me correct that: I was *told* about an experiment. One that was conducted by some research group. Government contractors, I think."

I check the room for any looks of recognition on the soldiers' faces, but I see none.

"The way I understood it—they way they told us—was that it was supposed to be some kind of psychological experiment, to see how people would react in the event of some global catastrophe. In this case, some nuclear Armageddon or something. They said they didn't really know the details."

"They?"

"They were two of the people inside the diner, the diner my friend and I fled to after the college."

"Your friend. Right."

I ignore the jab. "These people, they were part of the team—or maybe they were the team, I can't really remember—who were tasked with studying the effects of the people in the town once the blast went off. That's what they told us anyway, but, as you might have guessed, it didn't happen quite that way."

"That's pretty obvious," Smalley comments.

I nod. "It is, but still, they knew about a blast. They just thought it was going to be contained to our little college town. There was going to be a cordon, I guess, and then the army or CIA or whoever these people worked for were going to do the study. Gather the data or whatever. But the blast came a day early, and once that happened, they knew something was wrong."

"And you believed them?" Abramowitz asks. "You still believe all of what they told you? You think it was a mistake what happened here? What happened to the people who were out in the snow when it all went down?"

"I didn't say it was a mistake."

"But you believe they didn't know?"

I drop my eyes from Abramowitz and look out the window at the passing landscape. Jones seems to be navigating the road with little problem, which makes sense, since the snow is melting and the interstates should be mostly clear of traffic. Nobody would have stopped at this point in the highway when the snows came, not in the middle of nowhere. The few cars that we do pass are either smashed against each other or have drifted off to the side of the freeway. I assume this latter category is made up of drivers who left from some place close to the local exits shortly after the storm started and then changed into ghosts somewhere along the way.

"You got something to say there, Dom?"

I return my gaze to the soldier. "After we left the diner, on the way back to my house, one of the members of this research team—the man—had me pull off on one of the exits along the interstate. He said he had an emergency—a bathroom thing—but it wasn't..."

Abramowitz doesn't speak, allowing me to gather my thoughts.

"Against my better judgement, I pulled off, and then we got stuck in a snow bank just at the base of the exit. And then this guy, the research doctor, he starts to walk up to the gas station."

"Not a bathroom break though," Abramowitz says, shaking his head.

"Not quite. I followed him part of the way up the ramp, and then, at the top of the hill, this huge tank appears out of nowhere."

Instinctively, Abramowitz looks toward the two soldiers beside me, and I catch Jones' glimpse toward the back in the rearview mirror.

"Did I say something interesting, soldier?" I ask Abramowitz.

"What else?"

"It *was* an experiment the whole time, but not in the way we were told. It had nothing to do with our reaction to a blast."

"So what then?"

"I need to hear more about your story before I go on about what I know," I demand. "That's my deal."

Abramowitz gives a sideways glance toward the front, but his back is almost completely to Jones and the look never reaches the driver.

"Did you guys think this was some kind of psych ops thing? Like my friends were told. You must have had some questions about your mission, right? I mean, a whole county and more was being blocked off from the world and you guys never questioned why you were there?"

"We don't get paid to ask questions," Stanton says, as if reading a line from a bad action movie.

"Oh, please. Give me a break. Did you ever talk to colonel directly?"

"Who?" Stanton asks, and I see a similar look of confusion on Abramowitz's face. But Smalley looks away instantly at the mention of the colonel, as if she's been slapped in the face.

"No?" I ask, ignoring Smalley's reaction. "Not friends with the colonel then?"

No one answers, and I can see the conversation is deteriorating. I look away, back out the side window of the RV and ask "So how far can you go?"

Abramowitz narrows his stare in confusion and shakes his head. "What? What are you talking about?"

"I mean on the open road. How far can you go before you come to a blockade like the one on the Maripo River Bridge?"

"They didn't bother with blockades on this side of the river. At least not that I've seen. It's one thing to block off a couple of bridges in Warren County, but there's too much road out of this county. So they did something worse to keep us in."

"Worse than a blockade? What does that mean?"

Abramowitz stands still for a moment and then raises his head and stares at the ceiling. He then turns his back and walks slowly to the front of the RV and sits in the passenger seat next to Jones. He slumps low and stares out the side window.

I stare at him for a moment, waiting, and then I look back and forth to the soldiers beside me. "What just happened?"

The woman—Smalley—sighs and then stands up, seeming to be gathering her thoughts before taking one long stride to a captain's chair opposite of the couch on which Stanton and I continue to sit. She puts her hands over her face and then slides them up her forehead, straining her fingers through her hair.

She sighs again and then takes a peek back to the front before starting the tale. "There was a larger group of us when this first started. Ten of us to be exact. Soldiers who were abandoned and used as guinea pigs in this new snowy world."

"Ten? Wow. What happened to the rest?"

"Ten is too many people for one car. There's no sedan or SUV that can carry ten people—at least not comfortably. So we would travel in two separate cars. Always together, but separate, kind of caravan style."

"Okay."

Smalley frowns. "Well, of course, like I assume everyone did in the beginning, we started looking for the perimeter of this thing. Where did this nightmare finally end and the old world begin, right?"

I nod. It was the million-dollar question.

"It was the second day after the explosion, do you remember that day, the day the first round of snow stopped falling?"

I did remember. Of course. The day after. It's a day I would remember for the rest of my life. All that snow that fell that first day and night finally stopped. There must have been three feet on the ground. The group at the diner had quickly come to the conclusion that it was only that first day, that first snowfall just after the blast, that caused the changes. The people who went out in the snow that day were screwed, but the snows that followed—the ones that began again on the third day, were benign. At least so far.

I didn't know any of this when I was at the college, of course; Naia and I didn't see the crabs for several days after the blast. But Tom and Stella and Danielle saw them right away, and they figured out quickly how it worked. And Terry must have known the whole time.

"We ventured out to see what had happened," Smalley continues. "We were told about an experiment too—"

"Hey!" Abramowitz calls from the front, but his body language doesn't demonstrate the same force. He sits slumped, his fist screwed into his cheek as he continues to stare out the passenger window.

"Screw it, Bram," Smalley says calmly. "You're still holding on to some kind of honor for the people who left you? Or do you think if the world ever gets back to normal you're going to be hit with violating your clearance obligations?"

Abramowitz throws up a dismissive hand, defeated.

Smalley continues. "So yeah, we knew something was coming, and like your friends, we got a different version of what was supposed to happen. And then it all went to hell. At the time, we thought we'd genuinely gotten lost inside, that it was all an accident and a search was happening. We thought we'd be found within a day or two, so the group that had formed in the meantime went to investigate. To try to find out what went wrong and how we could help."

I have so many questions already that it's burning a hole in my chest. *What was their version of what was supposed to happen?* the most pressing of all. But I keep the questions to myself for the moment, not wanting to spook the storyteller.

"So we're driving the interstate, our caravan cruising, hauling ass, and eventually we come to a point, oh, I don't know, sixty miles or so west of where we are now, out where it's mostly country, and we start to see that the landscape is really beginning to change. Like really change. The snow suddenly was gone. There was none on the roads or trees. And we could see a whole mountain of foliage in the distance. Mountains that looked so green and alive against a blue sky. It was amazing the change, how stark and sudden it happened."

"Oh my god," I mutter. "I can barely remember what leaves look like."

Smalley nods. "I know. There were four of us at the time: Jones, Bram and I, and another guy Woodson. We hadn't met up with Stanton here yet. Anyway, we were in the trailing car, some piece of crap Toyota sedan, and the rest of the group was in the lead in an SUV. It could have easily been the other way around. There was no rhyme or reason to who was in the front when we went out, it was just kind of who left first, you know?"

I nod again, beginning to get the idea of how this story was going to end.

"The shell came from our right. We never even saw the tank or anything, just heard the pop of the main gun." Smalley swallows and closes her eyes for a moment and then opens them in a flash and continues. "And then we saw that fucking Durango just disintegrate. I mean, it was one of those moments, you know? Like you see in movies? Everything is going perfectly; some guy is having the perfect day, got the promotion at work or the girl's phone number or whatever, and then the dreaded news that's going to change everything comes from nowhere and lands like an anchor. Just yanks the freaking rug out from under him. And then his whole life is suddenly shit. That was us. Smiling and laughing, feeling good about our prospects ahead, and then boom." Smalley pauses again, this time seemingly for effect, before saying, "And then the machine guns started on us. Rat-tat-tat-tat-tat!"

"Holy crap," I whisper.

"Bram got us out. Me and Jonesy anyway. Woodson took a round in the neck. Nearly blew his head completely from his shoulders."

"Damn."

"Ever since then, we travel together. One car. And we got a ride big enough in case we pick up others along the way."

"So then you're not working with the colonel?" It's all I can think to say; I'm still mesmerized by the revelation of the story.

"What colonel?" Stanton asks.

I see ahead of me Abramowitz rise again and he's now walking back towards me with purpose. His face is stern, focused. "I think you must be ready to continue with your story, huh?" he asks rhetorically. "Now that you know all about our little family tragedy, I think it's time for your tit to our tat?"

I nod. "Yeah, of course. I'm sorry about your friends."

Abramowitz nods once to acknowledge my condolences. "So what about this plan you heard? The colonel's plan you heard on the road?"

"It was always about the crabs," I start, "the ghosts. Whatever. I don't know what you guys were told about the experiment, but according to the conversation I heard with the colonel, this whole thing was intentional. They knew the people would change. They knew it all along. And they wanted to see how they would behave afterwards. After the blast. They wanted to see if they would become violent, aggressive. But make no mistake: they knew these changes would happen. They just didn't know how they would behave over time, and this experiment, this destruction, was all a test to find out."

"How could you know about all this?" Smalley asks. "How could you know all of this unless you were a part of it?"

"I wasn't a part of it. For Christ's sake. I told you about the research doctor on the exit ramp. The one from the diner who wanted me to stop." I pause a minute and look back and forth between Abramowitz and Smalley.

"It's still your turn, professor," Abramowitz replies. "How do you know what you know?"

I frown. "I overheard this guy—Terry, the doctor—I heard his report to the colonel. At least I think he was a colonel, if my reading of his insignia was correct."

"And the colonel, he said this? He said the plan was about turning people into these things?"

"The research doctor said it. He said he had collected the data and that the theories were correct, that they became violent. That might not be the exact verbatim, but it's close enough."

"So what happened to him? This Terry person?"

I frown and think back to a couple of days ago and the violent end that Terry met. He wasn't my favorite member of the group, but his death still lingers in my mind, as does Naia's and Alvaro's. "He made contact too early, by several weeks apparently, and the colonel killed him for it. It sounded like an excuse to me; it sounded like Terry's death was always the plan."

Abramowitz nods slowly, his face showing signs of recognition, that this is the type of thing black ops folks would do.

"And that was when we had *our* encounter with the tank."

Abramowitz just stands in place for a moment, staring at me hard, as if processing all of the information I've just unloaded. "You were lucky to make it out, I guess."

"You have no idea...well, maybe you do. But yeah, we took a decent amount of fire." I sigh and shake my head, breaking out of my reverie, suddenly panicked again about the plight of Danielle and Tom and Stella and James. "Which is another reason why I need to find my friends. I've only known them for a couple of weeks and they've already saved my life more than once. I owe them. I need to get to a boat."

Abramowitz holds up a hand towards me, his palm out making a slow pressing motion. "Look professor, I'll uphold my end of this deal if that is what you still want to do. We're not far from the spot on the river where you left your friends. Near the bridge, right? So if you still want us to, Jones will drop you at a pier, you can rig a boat, and you can try to get out to them."

"Good, because that is what I want."

Abramowitz lets my words stand for a beat, staring into my eyes, searching for a deeper truth. He nods and says, "But I gotta tell you, and you said it yourself professor, they've been out there a long time. They either got that boat started or they didn't. Which means they either got out of there or they were overrun. And you venturing out into the river now isn't going to change that. It'll be dark in forty-five minutes. You trying to make it to the middle of the river now is a death sentence."

I look away, not ready to accept the logic of the soldier's words. Finally, I say, "I have to know. Either way I have to know what happened. So maybe you're right about getting out there tonight, but I at least need to get to the bank of the river and see if I can spot their boat from the shore."

"You won't be able to see anything in this light. You can barely see what's on the river at noon, let alone now, at dusk."

"Well what do you want me to do?" The words come out more forcefully than I intended, but my frustration and shame—shame at spending so much time in the Clam Bake, tending to my personal needs—is at a boiling point.

Abramowitz doesn't answer, but I know his belief is that I should let them go. At least for the night. And he's right, of course; by the time we reach a pier and find a viable boat with the keys inside—even if we get lucky and find it immediately—night time will be upon us. And with all the boats on the water, dark and impotent now that their masters have abandoned them, there's a better-than-average chance that I'll wreck the craft and drown in the freezing waters of the Maripo River.

Despite the anger I feel, however, mostly about my own ineptitude, the hope I feel for my friends is strong. They're a formidable bunch. Tom spoke as if he was comfortable on the water—far more than I, it seemed—so I'm confident he got the boat started somehow. And if he needed time, there was Danielle, who would hold off the crabs until he succeeded. I have to believe that.

"Fine," I say, filling in the answer to my rhetorical question. "We'll wait until tomorrow."

"It'll be too late tomorrow," Stanton pipes up.

"I need to know! You get that right? I just need to see if the boat is there or not. If it's been overrun or not."

"Okay, okay," Stanton says, rising now and heading to the bathroom at the back of the RV, leaving me alone now on the bench seat by the window.

Abramowitz frowns and looks to the ground before facing me again. "Look professor, I'm sorry, all right, but this is—"

"Where are we going?" I interrupt.

"There's a grocery store a couple of exits from here. It's secure and well-stocked. We make a run about once a week and were due."

I turn back toward the window and watch the landscape pass in a steady, seemingly endless, tableau of flat, empty ground. Only the occasional road sign appears sporadically, displaying the speed limit or the miles remaining to reach the next town.

And then, as if a giant blimp had suddenly been thrust from beneath the ground, the empty landscape becomes blanketed by a screen of white. I sit up straight now and take in the enormity of the cloud-white structure, a building which sits just off the interstate and stretches on for what seems like miles. I narrow my eyes and touch the tip of my nose against the glass, examining the structure like an architect. I've probably passed the building a hundred times, but something about it rivets me now, and I'm only really seeing it consciously for the first time.

The building is tall and curved like the shape of an airplane hangar, except it's so massive it's like several hangars that have been lined up side by side, forming an arched white tube that appears large enough to house a small village. I can't believe I've never given the construction a second glance, but it's so benign in terms of color and design, forming a steady border along the interstate, that it almost blends in with the horizon on either side of it.

The RV finally reaches what I believe is the front end of the structure and I turn my neck backwards, following it with my eyes as we pass, focusing now on the facade of the tube-shaped building.

And then I see the letters.

Painted in huge, faded blue script across the end face of the structure are the letters D&W.

D&W.

At first the writing has no effect on me, but my mind unconsciously takes in the blandly written print, and I look to the floor of the RV, my brain noting a grain of recognition that it wants me to locate.

"There are a couple of waterfront homes right at the base of the bridge," Abramowitz says, calling from the front of the RV and shaking me from my trance. "They all have boats. We'll get there early tomorrow and try to find one."

And then it comes to me. "Wait!" I yell. "Take this exit."

"The supermarket is off the next exit?" Jones says from the driver's seat; they're the first words he's said since we started driving.

"Did you see something, professor?" Abramowitz asks.

"Just get off here. Please. If I can't save my friends today, maybe I can get us some answers to what really happened here. Maybe find out who's responsible for it."

# Chapter 6

The RV pulls into the lot of D&W and I see instantly that what looks like a giant abandoned warehouse from the road is actually a functioning business. Or at least it was at one time, likely right up until the world came to a stop.

At the end of the caterpillar-shaped tube is a well-designed entrance with blonde wood paneling and windows that rise up about halfway to the roof where they join with a second story front-facing patio. It's quite gorgeous, actually, the design of someone with unlimited funds. It's a building you would find on the cover of an architecture magazine, though this whole section of the building is completely hidden from the interstate, a secluded gem in plain sight.

"What the hell is 'D&W,'" Smalley asks. "Sounds like some kind of root beer or something."

"That's *A&W*," Stanton replies.

"I just said it sounded like it."

Abramowitz stares at his two subordinates for a moment and then asks, "Are you two almost done?"

They both shrug and nod, and the four of us—Abramowitz, Smalley, Stanton and I—follow Jones, who is already standing at the base of the structure, staring up toward the roof. "How tall do you think this thing is?" he asks. "Seventy-five feet? A hundred?"

"It's damn tall," Abramowitz replies. "Could definitely fit a 747 under this thing. Can you imagine how much it cost to build?"

"No way this is some giant hangar though," Stanton says. "There's no airport or airbase anywhere close to here."

"Maybe they *build* planes inside," Smalley suggests. "You know, and then ship them off to somewhere else when they're complete."

"That could be," Stanton concedes.

I stare at Smalley and Stanton for a long beat, disbelieving, making sure they're serious about the possibility they've just constructed before offering the rebuttal. Finally, I say, "You two obviously are not from this area. Airplane factory? Are you kidding me? If this was an airplane factory it would be the biggest employer in five counties. Maybe the whole state. I pass this building all the time and never give it two looks—I think th at's how the designers intended it. But I know it's no airplane factory."

"So why are you looking now?" Abramowitz asks.

"What's that?"

"You said you never noticed this place. Why do you notice it now?"

I nod up towards the top of the building at the blue letters that hover above us. "D&W."

"What about it?"

"The letters were faintly written on the side of the building. I saw them from the interstate.

"So?"

"It's the name of the company where those scientists I was telling you about worked. The ones who were sent out to my college, ostensibly to observe the aftermath of the event."

"I thought you said they worked for the colonel," Jones says. "What do they have to do with this place?"

"No, I didn't say 'they' worked for anyone. I told you it was only the guy who was working with the colonel. The other one, the woman, she wasn't involved with him. At least I don't think so, though I think she might know more than she's admitting."

"Were you sleeping with her too?" Smalley asks.

I stare Smalley down and then say flatly, "No. And the truth is I could be wrong about all of it. I don't really know what's going on beyond the confessions of the scientists and what I overheard on the exit ramp. Except for this place. Stella mentioned the name of her company several times, and though she didn't know the full extent to which they were involved, they were definitely involved in the blast. I'm going to assume that much is true."

There are a couple beats of silence and then Abramowitz says, "Or maybe it's not."

I shake my head, confused. "Why not?"

"Maybe it was the colonel and his group who were behind the blast—who else would have the capability of firing off a rocket in the middle of an American county? But maybe it was this place that was behind the results."

"The results? What does that mean?"

"It means, that maybe these are the people that created...I don't know...the stuff that turned people into ghosts."

The soldier's words send a chill down my spine, a chill that feels familiar in my bones, familiar like the truth. Of course. It makes perfect sense. It was some shadowy military force that created the missile or bomb or rocket or whatever it was that detonated over the skies of Warren College that day, but it was D&W that made the chemical that turned the world white. A chemical company. That sounds right.

I walk up close to the large glass door of the warehouse and stare inside, but there is only a white wall staring back at me. A hallway leads to the right, presumably to the lobby of the mysterious building. "Yeah, maybe."

"So what do you want to do, professor?" Abramowitz asks. "Seems like a big task to go exploring a hundred-thousand square feet today. It's a good find though. Important even, I'm sure. But it's gonna be dark soon and, as domesticated as it sounds, I would like to get my grocery shopping done before it does. We can leave this for tomorrow. That and finding your friends."

I stare a few seconds longer into the building and then turn back to the group. "Sounds like a plan."

# Chapter 7

Night has fallen more quickly than Abramowitz estimated, and were now staring at the facade of Gray's Grocery and Tackle where, beneath the faded signs advertising the weekly discounts on meats and canned goods, blackness awaits us inside.

In the beginning, for the first couple of months after the blast, the snow had always acted as an illuminating agent, a white coating of reflection guiding the way like a lighthouse through our new world, a world which, other than that supplied by the occasional backup generator, contains no electricity.

But the snow has barely fallen in weeks, and the days have begun to grow warmer. Ever since the morning Naia and I made our escape from the student union, when the sun appeared for the first time in weeks and I'd agreed to leave, the temperatures have steadily risen. And now the blankets of snow, like that which covers the parking lot of Gray's Grocery and Tackle, have begun to melt, leaving a dark void where bright whiteness existed previously. My eyes work to adjust to this new lack of light.

I stand still in front of the store, noting the lack of snow or ice at my feet, feeling the tacky pavement beneath my boots. I depress the rubber button of my flashlight and unleash a strong beam forward. I'm in the back of the group, and my beam joins that of Abramowitz's who has cast his toward the front entrance.

"Turn that off," Abramowitz snaps. "There's enough light with mine. We don't need to advertise."

"Sorry," I whisper. "What's the crab count around here?"

Abramowitz shrugs. "We haven't' seen any of them at this particular store, probably because like the restaurant, there was an open door in the back when we found this place, so my guess is anyone inside eventually found their way out. But there's no need to bring extra attention to ourselves. Just in case."

I scan the other four in my group and note the lack of weaponry. "Guns might be a good idea, right?"

I notice Smalley first, not her face, but the nervous way she looks back and forth between Jones and Abramowitz. Something is wrong.

Abramowitz sighs. "We're out of ammo."

"What?"

"For about three days now."

"Out of ammo? But every one of you put guns on me back at the restaurant. What was that about?"

"Habit mostly. But also just a show. That's the thing about guns, professor. You usually just need to show them and people do what they're told. Works on humans pretty good. Not so much on those white sons of bitches."

"But you could find more weapons and ammo inside this cordon, right? I know it's not a big gun-owning community, but I've seen my share of weapons since this happened."

"Weapons yes. That's part of the reason we were out when we found you at that seafood joint. We were making a weapons run. But guns are getting harder and harder to come by. And we ain't gonna find ammo for those M-16s. Spent those rounds up quickly in the beginning. When they first came with the snow. Bullets don't last long. That's something you never see in movies."

"Well that might be a good first task tomorrow," I say, a tinge of sarcasm in my voice. "Not sure I want to go inside that warehouse with a penknife and a bunch of empty rifles."

"I'll put it on the list."

"Maybe we could finish this conversation inside," Jones says, surveying the parking lot. I can tell the lack of weaponry has him unnerved, and he feels naked in the darkness.

"After you, soldier," Abramowitz says, and we walk quickly to the front of the market, staying close to one another, trying to form a tight ball against the exposed night around us. Abramowitz pushes his chest against the glass entrance and wedges his fingers between the two sliding doors. He pulls them apart with little effort, and after we all step inside, he closes it back, pressing the edges together, making sure the rubber seals suck tight.

The grocery store is quite large, enormous, in fact, despite the folksy-sounding 'Grocery and Tackle' in its moniker. Even in the darkness, it's easy to see that the store was renovated, turned from a local market into something resembling a supermart, hoping to compete, no doubt, with the encroaching national retailers while still retaining its hometown name.

The first item that catches my eye is a tall cardboard tower, placed conspicuously inside the front door, where inside its hollow trunk is a bevy of silver and red snow shovels, blades sticking up over the lip of the box like baby birds waiting for their feeding. *Well that sure didn't take long*, I think to myself. Snow shovels in May? Who would even have those in stock? They probably had leftovers from the previous winter—a winter that was virtually snowless—and then figured they'd seize on the opportunity to unload them once the snow started to fall. What luck! But hey, how can you blame them? They couldn't have known what was coming. And if it had turned out to be just some freak, off-season snowfall, people would have needed a way to dig out. And Gray's would have been providing a much needed service.

Absently, I pick up one of the shovels in stride and carry it at my side like a staff, liking the weight of the thing in my hands, gripping the thick handle until I feel the burn in my knuckles.

The five of us enter the aisle furthest to our right—the produce department—and from what Abramowitz's flashlight displays, there isn't a single fruit or vegetable to be found.

He catches my gaze and says, "Most of it was spoiled by the time we found this place. Even with the temperatures what they were." He turns back and takes a wide scan of the store. "And speaking of things we should have waited until tomorrow to do...damn this place is dark at night."

"Told you this was not a good plan," Jones says, and then begins walking deliberately toward the seafood counter at the back of the store. He's out of range before Abramowitz can retort.

"Let's just get to the freezer and grab a couple of steaks," Smalley says, easing the light tension. "We've still got plenty of propane to get the grill going, so that's all we'll need to get us through the night. Tomorrow we can come back and do a more thorough shopping. Right after we check out that creepy hangar."

"Don't forget the guns," I remind her.

Abramowitz, Smalley, Stanton and I walk in the direction of Jones, who is now out of sight, navigating past the raised displays where everything from bananas and apples to cucumbers and kumquats were showcased not so long ago.

I bang my knee into a display case, one that is not symmetrical with the other platforms and seems ill-situated within the aisle. I stop to tend to the injury, gritting my teeth and holding back a four-letter word.

I look up to see that Smalley, Stanton and Abramowitz have now fanned out in the wide aisle and have reached the back of the store, and I limp forward in an attempt to catch up.

And then, as if something were waiting for my separation from the group, I hear a wet scurrying sound behind me, like the friction of skin on linoleum. I stop and turn my head toward the sound, the breath in my lungs turning to stone, frozen on the exhale. I turn my whole body now, my arms extended in front of me as I search the darkness in vain. I want to do nothing more than turn on my flashlight, but I resist, mostly from fear of what I'll see in front of me.

With my feet planted, I turn my head back towards the group and utter, "Hey!" hoping to garner the attention of at least one of my group. But they've moved too far ahead of me to hear, and my whispery grunt goes unnoticed.

I force my feet to pivot, and I turn back slowly in the direction of my group. I take my first step, then a second and third, moving hastily now, and I hear the slapping sound of skin again, this time off to my right. I stop again and pivot in that direction now, holding up the snow shovel with my right hand like it contains the power of Excalibur.

The sound continues, moving across the floor, behind me and then to my right, the sounds like the soles of a small child's feet on a kitchen floor sticky from spilled juice.

I follow the sounds with my neck, like I'm watching an invisible tennis match, and as the gruesome noise reaches the right side of the aisle again, a beam of light flashes toward it.

"What is that?" I hear Abramowitz ask from behind, and my feet instinctively turn and follow the direction of his voice, quickly bringing me into the sphere of the group.

"I don't know," I say, breathing for what feels like the first time in minutes, my voice whispery and scared. "It was behind me at first, and then off to my right. I think something is inside with us."

"Shit," Abramowitz says, and then, looking down the rear aisle that runs like a main street, extending the entirety of the back of the store, he asks, "Where the hell did Jones go?"

"I'm right here, boys," Jones replies, exiting the swinging back panel doors that lead to the bowels of Gray's Grocery, in his hand two plastic shopping bags, presumably filled with steaks.

"You know I'm a girl, right?" Smalley replies.

"You've certainly got the layout of this place down, haven't you?" Abramowitz says.

"I've made it a point to map the store out in my head. You know, for times like this, when 'we' make the decision to come here at night."

"Yeah, you're quite the industrious one, Jones. Maybe one day we can have a little fun challenge testing you on your Gray's Grocery knowledge. But not today. It seems the store has been breached."

Jones looks around. "Breached? By who? Where?"

"Don't know for sure, but I think we'd all have the same guess."

"Where is it?"

"We heard sounds in the produce section. Professor here says it was right behind him at one point. Haven't seen anything though. Just the sounds."

Jones nods in the direction of Aisle 2. "Well I guess that's that. We need to get outta here. We had a good run; this was bound to happen eventually. Guess it's time we found a new spot. Anyway, none of these places are gonna be viable much longer if it gets any warmer."

The five of us begin a quick walk down Aisle 2, and as we reach the main front aisle we convert the pace into a light jog, slipping through the first register and reaching our starting location at the front door.

Stanton leads the way and pulls apart the sliding doors to their full width, and with the entrance now fully open, he turns back to us, checking to ensure we're all with him and ready to go.

Abramowitz turns the flashlight toward the door, directly on Stanton, and, as if the beam itself triggered the reaction, Stanton's eyes flash open in terror and a muffled choking sound erupts from his mouth. His face is that of someone suffering a major heart attack.

And then I see them, just barely at first, and then as clear as day, the white fingers wrapped around Stanton's throat, clutching against the skin like tiny icicles, pressing against his thick neck, squeezing the breath and life and hope from the innocent young man. The rivulets of red are already flowing down the front of his neck and onto his chest.

Another hand then appears on top of the soldier's head, this one just as white as the one around his throat. And then, with the power of some assembly line machine, the hand pulls Stanton's hair up and back, violently yanking the man's entire body backwards and to the concrete ground outside the entrance of Gray's Grocery and Tackle.

Stanton hits the pavement with a gruesome thump, and the bottom halves of his legs—from the knees down—remain inside the store, his feet twitching convulsively.

"Grab him!" Smalley cries, the pain in her voice mimicking the look on her friend's face from only seconds ago. She makes a clumsy, desperate move toward the door.

"No!" It's Jones, intercepting Smalley before she takes her second step, hugging her towards him. "Look at him, Smalley, he's gone. There's nothing you can do."

Smalley slaps at Jones, trying desperately to push him off of her, tears now flowing from her eyes. "We can—"

"Look at him!"

Smalley lifts her head up and squints open her eyes, just in time to see the final section of Stanton—first name never known by me—dragged from between the sliding doors of Gray's Grocery and across the pavement toward the depot of shopping carts.

"Get your beams on," Abramowitz orders. "All of you."

Within seconds, the four flashlights are lit and shining out the front door of the grocery store, illuminating the north end of the parking lot.

The three of us don't see anything at first, other than the fallen body of Stanton and the crab that took him, the blood on the pavement beneath them an expanding lake of destruction. The crab is feeding on Stanton with veracity and pays no attention to the audience watching.

But then something in the distance starts to come into focus, just at the edge of the beams where the lines of the parking spaces begin, and I'm compelled to take a step forward, drawn to the movement like the sailors to the song of the mythical sirens.

"Are you crazy?" Abramowitz says, almost to himself, and then he barks, "Professor, get back here!" His voice is deep and gravelly now, the tone and cadence of a sergeant."

But I don't stop, because I know if I do, we'll all be dead in seconds. I see them clearly now. The growing vision on the perimeter of my flashlight is crabs. There's one in the front, alone, and then dozens of them behind, staggered in waves and moving toward us.

I reach the front and shine my beam through the open gap in the sliding doors, just to make absolutely sure that the horror I'm seeing moving steadily through the parking lot towards us is genuine and not some figment of my imagination.

But it's all too real. The white bodies and black eyes of the resurrected ghosts are moving like a small avalanche toward the entrance of the grocery store.

The first one—separated from the others by a good twenty yards or so—reaches the raised sidewalk in front of the store and passes Stanton's corpse without looking down. It's focused instead on the opening in front of him and, presumably, me.

Without thinking, I drop the flashlight to the ground, noting absently that it continues to shine despite the trauma it's just endured, and I grab the snow shovel tightly with both hands, duplicating the grip from earlier. The handle of the shovel is in my right hand; the fingers of my left hand are wrapped around the shaft about half way between the handle and the blade. I then extend my arms as far behind me as they will go, like I'm preparing a battering ram, pointing the steel scoop forward toward the opening of the door.

I don't have my own light anymore, but the group has kept theirs on the night outside, and I can see the crab approaching quickly. It's not running, but it is coming forward in a steady march, the look on his face as dead and detached as ever.

I grip the handle and shaft with the same amount of tension in each hand, keeping my focus on the strike, knowing that timing will be everything if I'm going to survive this encounter.

"Get the hell out of there, Dominic!" someone yells. I think it's Jones, but I can't tell for sure, so centered am I to the white beast before me. I hold my ground, spreading my feet apart about three feet, trying to get the perfect leverage.

"I've got him," I say, and somehow the confidence feels real.

The crab steps on the dead sensor mat of the automatic door and stops immediately in front of me, about two feet away. I can smell the vinegar coming off of it as it blinks twice and then pushes its head forward, birdlike, as if trying to investigate what is happening inside here without having to commit.

I don't waste a beat—I can see that the others following behind this one will be on me in seconds—and I bring the front edge of the shovel up and forward, landing the blade directly beneath the nose of the crab, feeling the push of the steel tip as it ravages the top of the crabs mouth and digs into the bone behind.

The crab shrieks and stumbles backwards, releasing itself from the grip of the scoop, allowing the blood from the wound to release and flow easily over its mouth. It takes several more steps back and then drops to its knees. It lingers in that position for several moments, only inches from the crab feeding on Stanton.

I instantly drop the shovel to the floor of the grocery and slam the doors closed.

And with not a second to spare.

In less than two seconds, three other crabs have arrived, disinterested in their fallen brother, curious only about what is taking place inside the building before them. They press their faces against the glass doors, staring.

I back away from the door and pick up my flashlight, and then I stare into the black pits that are examining me, looking for any sign of life or recognition from the monsters. A fourth face appears against the glass now, this one just as emotionless and disinterested as the others. Another follows, and then another, the faces filling in the pockets of glass until the entire door is a tapestry of white faces and black eyes, like a jumble of dice that have been glued to the inside of an aquarium.

I assume the crabs are blinded by the light, just as any human would be, but something in the way they watch suggests otherwise, and the black pearls seem to absorb it without effect.

I'm paralyzed, unable to move away. Even though only an inch of glass and a foot of space separate us, I feel like my stillness is somehow keeping them at bay. But it's more than that, I know. I'm stricken by them, held in place by their mere presence.

"Dominic!" Abramowitz calls.

Finally, I take a small step backward, never taking the beam of light off the door or the faces beyond it, moving the light from one face to another, waiting for the first crack in the door to appear and then the flood of white to overwhelm us. But it never comes. They just stand there staring, never making a move to pull the doors apart.

I work my way back to the group and stand beside Jones, who is now looking at me with some kind of mixture of fear and awe.

"Damn, soldier," he says to me, "that was like something out of *Lord of the Rings* or something."

I cock my head to the side and nod. "I guess. Just trying to live is all."

"What are we going to do?" Smalley asks, her grief momentarily subsided, her voice now sounding strong and willing. "I don't think we have enough shovels to lay 'em all out." She pauses. "But if that's the plan, I'm in."

"I don't think so," Abramowitz says. "And I know these things have problems with doors, but I can't imagine they won't figure it out and be in here in the next few minutes. Hell, they'll break the glass eventually." He looks over to Jones. "How many ways out of here?"

"There's a few. Emergency exits on both sides at the front and back. But we'll be exposed if there's any of them out there waiting. I think the best way out would be through receiving. Where the trailers pull in. The platforms outside are raised, so even if there are any of them out back when we walk out, they won't be able to get to us." He pauses. "It'd be better to wait until morning of course. Maybe they'll lose interest. We could wait it out and see."

As if on cue, the sound of slapping feet erupts again, this time somewhere between aisles five and seven. I'd already forgotten about that one.

"Guess you forgot about our new pet," Abramowitz says. "Don't think he plans on waiting it out."

"Maybe we can secure the front door somehow," Jones offers, not a trace of confidence in his voice. "And then hunt and kill whatever is inside."

"There's no way to secure that door," I say. "Even if we were in a hardware store and had those kinds of supplies. It's too unstable. I'm with Bram here: we have to go now."

Abramowitz checks the faces of the remaining group, looking for any other signs of dissent, and then says, "All right, let's go."

I begin walking with the group and then stop and head back towards the doors, again coming within a foot or two of the sea of monsters.

"What are you doing, Dominic?" Smalley asks.

I pull out three shovels and load them into the crook of my arm, and then I walk them over to the group, delivering them like swords before battle. "Just in case."

# Chapter 8

The receiving area at the back of Gray's Grocery is cold and sterile, with skids of wrapped grocery items—mostly paper products like paper towels and toilet paper—lined up along the concrete walls. At the very back of the large room is a giant door that opens ground to ceiling. This is where the truckers back their trailers in so their cargo can be unloaded directly into the store.

"Don't you need power to open that thing?" Smalley asks. "Looks like a giant garage door."

"That is what it is," Jones replies. "And it would certainly be easier that way. But in case you hadn't heard...anyway, it's got a manual option." He nods to some type of metal pulley system that runs vertically along the side of the door.

"Okay then," Smalley says, "let's get to it."

Jones makes his way to the pulleys and wraps his hands around the chain. "We're only going to open it as far as we need to. I have a feeling this door is going to be loud, and I'd rather those things not make their way around to the back. Obviously."

Jones looks toward the door that leads from the shopping area to the back room where we stand currently. Abramowitz is standing guard.

"Any signs of a breach?"

Abramowitz frowns and shakes his head. "No. Haven't heard from our visitor in a while either."

"What's the plan once we make it out?" Smalley asks.

"There's three trucks out back. I doubt any of them have the keys inside, but we can at least hide there until morning if we have to."

"And what if they're still there in the morning?"

"I don't know, Smalley. Then I guess were screwed. But we definitely don't want to spend another minute in here, so once I pull this door up, who's gonna be the first one out?"

"I'll go," I say, not hesitating. "Are you sure you can raise that thing by yourself?"

"I can raise it. Don't know how long I can keep it up though."

"Bet your girlfriend gets tired of hearing that," Smalley says without a smile, as if the joke was obligatory, even if she didn't have the heart behind it.

Jones snickers. "Here goes, Professor. Make sure you have your flashlight. And keep that shovel handy. Just in case."

I pat the space in my pants where the flashlight is stashed and hold up the snow shovel. I'm ready.

Jones unlatches the large, crescent-shaped door lock and then grabs the chain and pulls down, straining as he leans backwards, his back nearly horizontal with the ground. At first there is barely a squeak from the rusty gears, but then, with one last Herculean pull, the bottom of the door cracks open, just enough to allow in a thin ray of moonlight and a gust of cool air.

"Give me a hand here, Smalley." Jones' says, barely able to grunt out the sentence.

"Damn it. Sorry Jones. Hang on."

Smalley moves in and places her hands on the chain above Jones,' and then pulls down in unison with him. I'm waiting at the narrow gap that was just created, lying on my belly now, waiting for the space to open just wide enough to squeeze under.

The door creeps open another couple inches, and Jones takes a deep breath and says, "Remember, once we've got this bitch up and you're outside, there should be a whole stack of milk crates lined up out there. I saw them there when we first canvassed this place, so there's no reason they aren't there now. Those things are strong as iron. As quick as you can, just slide one of them underneath. We'll hold up the door as long as we can. And if the coast is clear, we'll be right behind you."

I give a somber nod and then Jones and Smalley give the pulley one final yank down, and the door opens wide, like a giant mouth, creating the gap I've been waiting for.

"Go!" Smalley says.

I toss the snow shovel out first and then follow right behind it, rolling out to the concrete landing. I give myself an extra two rolls for cushion, making sure to get far enough away to clear the door.

I'm out.

I'm blind for a moment, but my eyes adjust quickly to the night, and I can see the blue latticework of the milk crates just off to my left.

I hurry to my feet and link my fingers through one of the crates, and as I begin to carry it back to the door, ready to place it underneath, I hear the screams and the clicking retreat of the gears to the door lift.

I rush toward the door with the crate out in front of me, but it's too late: the giant metal gate closes with a boom to the concrete, leaving me standing like a beggar on the wrong side of it.

I stare in disbelief at the metal barrier, scanning the area for a pulley system that would enable me to lift the door from this side. But of course there is nothing, and my mind begins to race with panic, both at the prospect of being stranded outside with the crabs, and my imagination about the chaos happening inside. I don't have context for the screams, and I want to believe someone banged his shin on a raised pallet, but logic tells me Abramowitz, Jones and Smalley are being ravaged by crabs.

I step to the door and put my ear against the metal barrier, hoping to decipher the sounds of mayhem behind it, but there is only silence now, and I have no way of knowing if the quiet is due to the thickness of the door, or if it's because everyone inside the receiving area is dead.

I bang on the door with my right fist and begin screaming the names of each of my companions, my panic now spilling over into despair. There's no answer.

I step back from the receiving gate and place the palms of my hands across my face, taking in a few deep breaths, trying to calm my nerves so I can think of what to do next. But I can't get calm; I'm sweating prolifically and my heart is racing like a nervous rabbit's.

"Dammit, Dom, relax. Standing here scared isn't an option. I have to get back to the RV. There's no ammo, but there has to be something inside I can use as a weapon. That's the goal now. Get back to the RV and get it started."

The trucks.

Jones mentioned three tractor trailers that would be parked out back, and I take note of the large rigs for the first time.

I grab the shovel and hop down from the concrete receiving platform and on to the street, and then rush over to the first truck in the row, scurrying up into the cabin of the tractor unit. I flick on the flashlight and search the front part of the cabin, and then start sifting through the sleeper cabin behind.

The sleeper cabin is basically an area carved out to allow enough room for a cot to be placed inside, but there is also shelving above the cot and storage space at the foot, each of which contains a variety of items. My search is far from thorough, since time is pressing on me like an iron, but I can tell immediately that there's not much here that is visibly usable. Clorox wipes. Books. A half-pack of cigarettes. A further search turns up a few snack size Doritos bags, and beneath the cot a thick nylon bag with the words "Roadside Kit" written in red lettering on the side.

I grab the chips and (for some reason I can't explain, since I don't smoke) the cigarettes, as well as the emergency kit. I forego inspecting the contents of the kit for the moment, and instead I exit the cabin of the truck and move on to plunder the other two, doing a quick search of each, increasing my stash of junk food and cigarettes, as well as finding a nice-looking bowie knife and several pairs of gloves. None of these items add up to the Holy Grail of supplies, but they're something, and though I'm sure there's much more to be found in the more secluded compartments of the cabins, I simply don't have the time now. But I'll take it. You never know when something will come in handy.

I hop down from the third and final truck and make my way hastily toward the corner of the building, at the intersection where the back wall of the store meets the side wall. I stop at the junction and peek slowly around the side, and, seeing that the path is all clear—at least to the end of my limited vision—I jog the length of the wall until I come to the next corner, the junction where the side wall and front facade meet. I peer down the length of the front of the store now and I can see them; the crabs that were at the door when we fled to the back of the store are still standing there, milling around, pressing their white bodies against the glass of the non-working automatic doors.

I turn from the mass of white flesh and look off into the lot, where a sea of white bodies are still emerging, piercing through the night in a steady wave, continuing to flow in the direction of the store. There must be a hundred of them now huddled at the front.

The first of the crabs that came, the one that took Stanton and the ones just after, must have been in the area at the time we arrived at the store and seen us exit the RV. Or maybe they were even closer than that and heard us speaking in the parking lot or closing the door of the vehicle. Or maybe they saw the light in the store.

Or maybe they smelled us. I've never really considered that sense when analyzing these creatures.

But the rest of them, the crabs that continue to descend upon Gray's Grocery, they can't know about us. They're simply reacting to the flow of the others, who are reacting to the ones already at the store. They have to be. They can't have any clue as to why their un-dead fraternity is huddled up against this dark building.

I think of the bridge now and the hundreds of white ghosts that were perched upon the ledge. Nothing attracts a crowd like a crowd, I guess. That idiom rings true to the sight I'm seeing now, and I have a feeling it would apply to the bridge as well. I don't know what brought them all there to the South River, but something must have led one to start, and then a million more followed. And then they were trapped there by the barriers. Could it be they were lured to the bridge, purposely drawn to it as a trap? How else would they have all been there when the bridges were cut off?

The thought sounds both crazy and obvious at the same time, but I don't have the luxury to chase the theory further, so I file it away for a later time. At least I know now the front door of the grocery store hasn't been breached, and that whatever screams I heard just as the receiving door was coming down was likely caused by the crab that was already inside. I'm guessing three roughnecks could deal with one crab, but there could have been more inside, others in different aisles that we didn't see. In any case, they could still be alive and trapped at this very minute. It's an assumption I have to make, and one that compels me to find a way to help them.

My stomach is tied up in terror as I walk away from the corner of the building and the cover of the brick wall that forms the side of Gray's grocery. I feel naked after only a few steps, but I keep my eyes focused, straight ahead on a dark lamppost that I estimate to be no more than twenty yards in front of me.

The pairs and trios of crabs continue crossing the parking lot, moving straight ahead, as if on a rope, drawn to their brethren like paper clips to magnets. Their narrow focus is my only hope of making it through the first segment of my journey; as long as I stay quiet, I'm pretty sure I can get to the post unnoticed.

Once there, however, I'll need to cross to the RV, and that will prove much more difficult. But for now, I just need to get away from the store and get through stage one.

I pick up my pace now, increasing it from a walk to a steady lope, and within seconds I'm across the open space of lot with my back against the pole of the lamppost. Only the furthest width of my shoulders is exposed, and I stand like a soldier in a fire fight behind the black pole, turning my head like an owl as I peek back to the action, measuring the crabs, assessing the distance between me and the RV.

The vehicle is parked smack dab in the middle of the lot, like it's the hub of Gray's parking system, exposed like an island in the eye of a hurricane while a steady stream of crabs approach it like an unstoppable tropical wind.

I know now I'll never make it there by simply running to it, at least not until the crabs stop coming, and I can't possibly know when that will be. I need a distraction.

I slow my breathing down again, and, slowly, my mind follows. I don't have much to work with in terms of options, but I come up with a plan to draw the crabs' attention away, if only for a few seconds.

I step away from the post and grip the handle of the shovel with both hands, making sure to keep the post in line between me and the crabs. But I'm in the open now, and without hesitation, I hold the shovel down by my hip and then spin once, turning a full revolution, and then release the snow shovel back towards the store. I restrain the grunt that forms in my throat, but the toss is well-delivered, hurled like a hammer throw at a track and field meet. I stop and follow the shovel with my eyes as it sails through the night, pleased at my technique and the distance it travels.

The clanging sound on the pavement is louder than anything I could have hoped for. It sounds like a steel trashcan being dropped from a five-story building. I look back to the crabs in the parking lot that are flowing toward the store, and can see that for the first time their attention is diverted. They've all stopped dead in their tracks, their heads turned toward the sound.

I continue to stand several feet back from the lamppost, still exposed to the night, and for a moment I think the crabs will look right at me, in search of the source of the noise, the way any thinking person would. But after a few beats of stillness, the crabs begin walking toward the side of the building, heading to the location of the noise itself, never once turning their heads in my direction. I look back to the crabs at the front door and see that the ones at the back of the pack have begun to move toward the corner of the store as well, drawing with them those closer to the interior of the mob. Within seconds all the crabs are moving to the shovel in a steady migration.

I look behind the crabs still in the parking lot but I can see only night—there are no white bodies flowing in behind them. I don't have the luxury to believe that I've seen the last of the waves, but for now there's a gap. Another pair of them will be coming soon, I have no doubt about that, so if there is ever a time to go for it, now is it.

I take a deep breath and then break into a sprint.

I keep my head down and at first bolt in the direction away from the store, and then, once I've gone about twenty yards, I make a sharp right turn and beeline in the direction of the RV. The twenty yards up is probably overkill, but I need to ensure I've created a wide enough berth to avoid the crabs in the lot that are now heading toward the corner of the store. The moon has ducked behind the clouds for the moment, so from this position I can no longer see any of them. But I can still hear the sickening wet patter sound on the blacktop, like giant rodents running toward a meal in a sewer main.

I'm about halfway between the lamppost and the RV, starting to gain a morsel of hope, when I hear the sound of footsteps coming from a different direction. The sound no longer is coming from in front of me in the parking lot, but instead beyond the perimeter of the store property, from the freeway. As I expected, the next wave is coming, and I'm directly in the path.

I stop in place, frozen for the moment, and still a good twenty-five yards from the RV. But I have to know my options, so I hold my breath and listen, trying to gauge if this new wave of crabs is headed toward me or whether they've caught the scent of the mob and are following the mass of bodies toward the shovel. It's a delicate distinction, trying to place the direction of footsteps, and despite my wishful thinking, my honest assessment tells me they're headed at me.

I'm trapped now, and I want to scream, but I keep my focus, figuring if I'm going to die, it's not going to be because I panicked. I reach for my waistband, and for the first time since arriving here, I pull out the flashlight and shine it directly into the night toward the sound of the approaching footsteps.

There's nothing at first, and I drift my aim back and forth slowly, searching the blackness, expecting monsters with every illumination. Reluctantly, I turn the beam in the direction of the corner of the building where I threw the shovel, and I can see that the entire crowd of crabs has convened to that side of the building. Regardless of how this ultimately turns out, that part of the plan worked perfectly.

I consider that perhaps I've misjudged the oncoming footsteps, that without the normal ambient sounds around me, I don't have the same sense of direction and location. Buoyed, I turn the flashlight back toward the edge of the parking lot for one more look. And now I see them.

The new wave, how many exactly I can't tell, but they're no more than ten or fifteen yards away, growing larger with each step as they flow through the beam directly towards me.

My instincts kick in and I immediately start running toward the RV.

A race of death has begun.

Since I tossed the shovel, I don't have a weapon at my immediate disposal; the knives I scavenged from the trucks are stuffed in a bag and not readily accessible to use at the moment. It wasn't great planning on my part, stuffing them away like that, but here we are.

The crabs are close enough to smell now, but I keep the beam fixed on the RV, the passenger door growing ever closer in my sights, almost enough to give me hope. A few more strides and I'll be there. I may not have time to open the door and get inside, but at least I'll have some cover from the vehicle. I may have to maneuver around it a bit, using it as a defense until I can trick my way inside, but at least I'll have a chance.

But that whole plan suddenly falls to pieces.

Two of the crabs, whether by their own dumb luck or, more frighteningly, through some primitive intelligence, dart into the path of the light and stop, staring down the length of the beam, separating me from my destination. They stand shoulder to shoulder in the light at the side of the RV as if waiting for a ride.

I let out a half yelp and stop in my tracks, almost falling forward towards them. I look into the cold faces and can see that their eyes are as dead as always, their faces blank. But the one crab on the left has its mouth slightly open, almost smiling, and I can see the viciousness waiting behind the lips.

The footsteps that were slapping at me from behind stop at the same time I do, and, now remembering that danger, I pivot, swinging the beam of light behind me. I can see the third crab is standing and staring, keeping a bit more than an arm's length distance, its blank eyes staring at me like I'm a child. This one's mouth is closed and flat, showing no interest in destroying me, despite what I know its instinct to be.

Every few seconds, I swing the light from my back to my front, illuminating the two crabs standing by the RV, and then back to the one behind me, using the light like some type of weapon from a sci-fi movie, minus the deadly effects, of course.

I'm trapped, dead likely, and with that thought, the crab from behind takes a step forward.

I move closer to the RV and the two crabs waiting there, still a little over two yards from their clutches. I could run back toward the store, but I know the distance is too great. I've seen them move, and I'll be run down before I make it half-way there.

The crab behind takes another small step toward me, and I know it's only a matter of seconds until this is all over. I can smell the ammonia as it moves in, and for just a moment I resign myself to death, figuring that making it this far has been nothing short of a miracle. It has to end sometime.

I turn my body so that the crabs are on either side of me now, and I take a step to my right toward the RV, slowly running out of real estate.

I think of the bridge again, and the student union at Warren Community College, recalling the behavior of these white devils, knowing that they can calculate their kills like generals, despite their more savage instincts once the prey is right in front of them.

The moment of truth has arrived. I can quit now and be dead in seconds, or I can keep fighting until the end.

I conjure some deep fury within me and scream toward the single crab at my left, almost barking at it like a cornered hound. The crab flinches back, which I accept as a positive sign, that they have the capacity for some level of fear, and with it momentarily stunned by my resistance, I crouch to the ground and drop the nylon emergency kit on the street in front of me.

I place the flashlight on the ground with the beam facing the lone crab, but I force myself not to look at it, focusing instead on the contents of the roadside kit, knowing my only hope is a miracle.

And there it is, nestled against the side of the rectangular case between a set of jumper cables and a can of tire sealant.

A flare.

I pull the dull red wand from its pocket and twist off the top, and then with a quick snap of my wrist, strike the flare against the course surface of the cap.

A sparkle of light appears like magic, like something from an animated fantasy movie, crackling and shining in the dark night like some kind of miraculous invention. Still stooped, I raise the flare above my head, energized now with a new sense of power, feeling like the first caveman who found fire and presented it to his Neanderthal mates, soon to become the first god of humans.

I pick up the flashlight again and stand up straight. I find the face of the lone crab and see its once-dormant expression has now twisted into a crumple of pain and fear. I hear grunting sounds behind me and swing the light toward the crabs at the RV. Their faces are equally as tortured as the crab opposite them, and, for the first time, I take an intentional step toward them, holding the flare in front of me.

The two crabs guarding the RV squint their eyes and bow their heads to the side, as if trying to watch the flare and resist it at the same time. I lunge at them, thrusting the flare toward their torsos, and they nearly stumble over each other in an attempt to keep away from the menacing crackle.

The two crabs have cleared the hood of the RV now and are heading toward the store. I keep the flashlight on them until they're twenty feet or so away, and then I turn back to the crab that was behind me. That one is also retreating, keeping its eyes fixed on the flare like it's a vial which contains the potion capable of its ultimate destruction.

Perhaps that's exactly what it is, I consider, and then bring my focus back to the moment.

I run at the crab now, no longer measured in my attack, and as I do, the human look of anguish increases on the crab's face; the frown of its mouth and wrinkle of the brow as indicative of fear and pain as any I've ever seen.

"You want some of this, asshole?" I ask. My voice is calm now, as if my question were legitimate.

I take another step at it and it turns away fully now. I keep my beam on it as it begins running toward the front of the store. It looks back once as it retreats, and I can see the beam of the flashlight catches the glint of its teeth, sending a shiver up my back.

I don't really know how long these flares last, and I only saw the one inside the kit; but I make a note that if and when I get out of this jam—which is looking like a much better prospect than it did less than a minute ago—I'll head back to the rigs to look for more. And surely the grocery store has some. And other things that light up.

They hate fire. The thought suddenly comes to me like a message from the ether.

Of course they do. They're snow monsters. If I was a snow monster, the one thing I would definitely hate is fire.

I open the door to the RV and step inside, clutching the keys from the dashboard and turning on the vehicle, still holding the flare in my left hand, now feeling almost invincible with the torch in grasp.

But before I start the engine, I de-press the button to roll down the passenger side window, at first just a crack, and then fully. And I listen.

There's only silence now—no sounds of footsteps or flowing hordes, no clamoring for position at the head of the door to Gray's Grocery. I turn on the headlights of the RV and they light up the large pane of glass that forms the front window of the store, as well as the front door. There isn't a single crab still standing on the sidewalk between the shopping carts and the door; only the dismembered corpse of Stanton remains.

I start the engine now and put the RV into drive, moving it slowly forward as I turn the wheel to the right, angling it so that the headlights are shining in the direction of where the group of crabs descended on the shovel.

Not surprisingly, they're still there—maybe seventy of them now—each one stooping like monkeys, staring at the oncoming RV. I can't know by simply studying the expressions on their faces, or even through their body language, but there is a sense of fear emanating from the pack now—even dread—as I approach.

I pull the RV a few yards closer, and then closer still, and finally, before the crabs in the front begin to feel the push of the giant steel grill, the pack begins to move backwards, quickly now, nervously, never taking their eyes away from the vehicle.

The RV is enormous, and I could obviously run several of them down with almost no effort, and do quite a bit of thinning of the horde's numbers before they ever had a chance to retaliate. But still, I don't think it's the brawn of the RV that has made them start to retreat. After all, we've been driving past crabs since we left the Clam Bake—and my group from the diner and I drove past dozens of them in our box truck—and most of them paid us little mind.

But I already know what it is they see. I know exactly what the source is of their growing terror.

I put the RV in park and leave it running, headlights shining brightly on the pack of white bodies in front of me, the crabs all huddled together tightly like a mischief of rats.

I grab the satchel containing the Bowie knives and place my flashlight inside of it, and then I open the door and step down from the RV. I reach the pavement and hold the flare out like an offering to the crabs, daring them to take the gift.

Almost the second I lift the flare in front of me the first of the crabs—those furthest away from me, in the back of the horde—begin to flee, scattering like beetles into the trees on the north border of the store and the interstate to the west, the direction from which these crabs all came originally.

And then the chain reaction occurs.

The next layer of bodies from the back begins to dissipate, and then the next, and suddenly the sea of white becomes a sprinkle in the black night, a light dusting of confectioner's sugar atop a cake of dark chocolate.

Until finally there are none.

I follow the last one, casually walking in its wake as it runs from the store toward the interstate, watching it as it drifts out of the range of the headlights. I turn back to the store to see little evidence that any of them had ever been there at all. Other than the body of Mr. Stanton.

I do a quick check around the side of the building, just to make sure there are no lingering crabs who may have wandered off to the back of the store during the chaos. But it's a formality, really; I already know the answer. I'm beginning to understand how it works now. Just as the crabs are drawn by other crabs towards the action, so too do they flee danger with the pack. And with the flare still shining brightly, and likely capable of being seen for miles, I have little to worry about for the moment.

With the parking lot and the surrounding area now empty, I head back to the front door of the store, passing the body of Stanton as I go. I don't look down at him. It feels like a cold move on the surface, as inhuman as the crabs that killed him, perhaps, but there's nothing to do about it now and only time to waste.

I pull open the automatic doors and push my way inside, and immediately run toward the back of the store and the receiving area where I last saw the remaining survivors of my new group.

I glance at the flare as I lightly open the swinging door and notice it's starting to diminish, but I hold it out boldly, expecting to see carnage and chaos, preparing to fend off an attack. With the flare dwindling and three people in distress, four including me, I can't be overly cautious; whatever I decide to do once I get through these doors will need to be done with haste.

I see the blood first, a sparkling pool of it shimmering in the halo of the fading flare, puddled at the threshold of the back room. Behind the puddle is a long slick that trails back into the rear of the receiving room.

I look to the left of the pool now and see a lone boot lying on its side. Sticking out of the top of it is the lower half of a man's leg; judging by the length of the bone and crooked fragments, it looks to have occurred somewhere mid-shin.

I put my hand to my mouth, stifling what was sure to be some hybrid of a scream and a gag, and I force myself to march further in, my head on a swivel. I fumble in the satchel and pull out the flashlight now, and then click it on nervously with a press of my thumb.

The beam explodes forward and the first thing that appears is a pair of eyes. Not the black eyes of death, but light brown, human. They're wide, disbelieving, and framed above and below, left and right, by long, thick bars of metal shelving.

"Oh my God, it's Dominic!" a voice calls from behind the bars. It's Smalley, and I can see the fear in her eyes has been diluted slightly with hope.

"Dom?" It's Jones now, his voice sounding almost delirious, disbelieving. I can't see any part of him from where I'm standing, but his voice is coming from the same general area of Smalley's. "Watch out, Dom. It's...I think it's behind that stack of pallets by the loading door. It's trying to find a way in here."

I move into the room a few more steps, trying to get my bearings as to what type of contraption Jones and Smalley are in exactly, wondering where the creature is trying to enter. I note the stack of pallets Jones has just referred to, and then I start to place the pieces together. Jones and Smalley have created a metal protective cage using three or four industrial trailer carts, the kind that come from the warehouse to the store, loaded to the top, full of supplies waiting to be unloaded. These carts are empty, but the structure is effective. Their arrangement is like some kind of small prison, Smalley and Jones the inmates, intent on keeping out the ghostly warden milling around the outside.

"Where is Abramowitz?" I ask, looking to the stains on the floor.

There's silence at first, and then from Jones, "He's in here. He's alive, but he's bad."

I assumed the boot was Abramowitz's; he was the one standing guard by the door when I left.

"Holy Jesus, Dominic," Smalley says, "I can't believe you made it out. And that you're still alive."

"I can't believe you came back," Jones adds soberly. And then, "There's a shovel just to your left, right beside these carts. If that thing—"

Before Jones can finish his plan, I hear the crab scurry from behind the pallet and I catch it immediately in the beam of the light, lucky to have detected it before it got too close. I take a step forward, gripping the flare like a samurai sword, horizontally in front of me, the flashlight pointed low and straight.

"Dom what are you doing? It's too late to get the shovel now. Just get out of here and find another weapon. This coop is pretty good. We can hold that thing off for a few minutes longer."

"I have a weapon," I say, and then I take another step forward.

The crab stares at me for a beat, but then, as instinctually as the others did when I stepped down from the RV just a few minutes earlier, it begins to walk backwards, lurching, ungraceful in its movements. The wrinkle of terror that shone in the eyes of the outside crabs appears above the one I've got in my sights now.

And for this crab, there is nowhere to run. He's trapped.

It starts to move quickly now, stumbling over its bare feet, and then it turns to run forward and, not seeming to understand its environment, slams shoulder-first into the giant receiving door, the rattle of metal ringing through the cavernous room like a gong.

The crab loses its footing and falls to the ground, slipping at first as it scrambles back to its feet, wheezing in fear, growling in terror at no one in particular.

"Dom!" Smalley screams.

I'm only a foot away from the crab now when it finally looks up at me, its expression morphing entirely into anger as it bears its teeth, threatening.

"Bring it, bitch," I say, barely whispering as I mouth the words.

The crab lunges at me, erupting from its crouching position like some giant albino frog, its arms stretched, fingers grasping as it reaches for my throat.

I feel the cold tips of thin fingers brush against my Adam's apple, but they never find their aim. I dodge them with a confident bob of my head, narrowly escaping the grip of the crab's talons as I lean back, my feet never moving from their spot, avoiding the full reach of the crab's arms like a boxer avoiding a wild left hook.

The crab stays on its feet, and its momentum sends it stumbling toward me. But having missed its mark, it's now off balance, out of control, and almost falls face first. It places the palms of its hands on the floor to stay upright, and I turn toward it, pivoting so that the back of the crab's head is now directly below me. For an instant it looks as if the creature has bowed before me in defeat.

But that isn't what the position means at all. There is no submission coming from this monster. Feeling trapped, unable to escape the fire of the flare, its only instinct now is to kill the threat. To kill me. And I can see in the veracity of its movements that it will continue to fight until either I'm dead or its path to safety is clear.

But I have no intention of allowing the beast to leave, and I'm willing to take the challenge to the death. But I know it won't come to that. Not today. I've discovered something. I know something about their weakness that I didn't know an hour ago. A new hope has sprung up within me, a new hope about survival and escape from this prison camp of Warren and Maripo County.

And the only way I can be sure that my new weapon is as powerful as these creatures would lead me to believe is to use it.

These thoughts all occur in a fraction of a second, and the crab is still bent down in front of me, its face to the ground, exposing the back of its skull and neck to the sky. Finally, it turns its head up slowly toward me, inhumanly twisting its neck until the ghost's eyes are staring up at me, shimmering in their sockets, vibrating with anger.

I see the tension in its thighs as it makes a move to stand straight, to lift its head back up to eye level. Its mouth is fully open, teeth chomping like a piranha, exactly like the crab locked in the cage of the gift shop.

Without an utterance or a breath or a single moment of doubt, I plunge the flare down into the thing's forehead, stabbing the sizzling fuse directly between the crab's eyes. And then, with the strength and will of demonic possession, I twist the tip of the flare back and forth, drilling it as far as it will go into the beast's head, finally extinguishing the flare on the surface of the crab's skull like a giant cigarette.

I rotate the stick of fire several more times, even after the crab's destruction is inevitable, just for good measure. But there is only silence now. There are no sounds of screaming or growls of rabidity; there is only the burning sound of flesh devouring the final cells of life that still remain.

But the crab isn't dead. Not yet. What the creature has abandoned vocally, its face displays in the form of true pain. It flails its arms desperately toward its head, trying to locate the source of the pain, but not quite able to find it.

I stop rotating the flare and then push on it with all my weight, forcing the crab down onto its back before finally releasing the tube of death.

The crab's arms still wave impotently over its face, but the eyes of anguish and facial expressions of disaster are gone. It has reverted back to its default manner of being, cold and lifeless, detached from the horrors of its situation.

I stand up straight and stare down at the red cylinder that now rises from the center of the crab's face like a rocket ship, one that has crashed on the surface of the moon perhaps, the black burn mark in the center of the crab's head the crater.

There are a few more timid waves of the crab's arms before it finally drops them to the side where they smack to floor like wet eels. These are the final movements of the thing before it finally dies.

And then something bizarre begins to happen.

The round black crater mark in the center of the crab's head begins to grow, the entire circumference of the ring expanding on the crab's forehead like an oil slick in the ocean. There's no more heat coming from the flare—the flame has been extinguished by the blood and fluids inside the crabs head—but the damage created by the fire seems already to have been done. I continue to watch the spreading virus of char, which has now covered the cheeks and chin and neck of the crab. Within seconds, the entire upper body of the dead beast is as black as coal.

And it continues to spread.

I hear footsteps behind me and I pivot toward them, my arms raised in a kung fu pose, flashlight in hand, ready to take on the next crab in line, now feeling a particular sense of power over this new species of murderers.

But it's only Jones and Smalley that have arrived. They've extricated themselves from their makeshift fortress and are now standing beside me, watching the growing disintegration of the crab lying at my feet.

"Damn professor," Smalley says, "you got a knack for this. You're like Van Halen or something."

"I think you mean Van Helsing?"

"That's what I said, right?"

"We have to go," Jones says, not offering his comments on any of the events that just occurred over the last few minutes. He lowers his voice a notch. "We have to get Bram to a doctor."

I return my gaze to the crab and am instantly mesmerized by the sight. The burn created by the flare has consumed the entirety of the crab, and it begins to fall apart—quite literally—its face and entire upper body now little more than a pile of ashes.

"Dom, did you hear me? Bram needs a doctor now."

"What doctor?" I ask, barely processing the words, confused and saddened by the impossibility of the statement.

"I don't know. We need to try to find one though. He's dying."

I break my fixation on the crab and walk with Smalley and Jones over to where Abramowitz is sitting up against the rear of the trailer cart. He's still conscious; his eyes are open and he's breathing, albeit with great effort.

Jones and Smalley somehow managed to tie off the wound with a tourniquet—a feat that I'm astounded by, given the fact that they were being hunted during the process—but there is still an extraordinary amount of blood beneath Abramowitz's severed leg. And sweat falls off his face in large drops, like a tropical waterfall, despite the chilly air that hangs in the receiving room.

He lifts his head, struggling to meet my eyes, and when he does, I look away.

"Doesn't look good, does it professor?"

I look back at him, locking in on his stare, feeling it's the proper thing to do for a military man at the brink of his death. And it's also proper to tell the truth. Or at the very least not lie. "No it does not, Bram." My voice is stern, unsympathetic. "But there's no sense losing hope. There's some good news: I cleared the storefront. Got all those sons of bitches to flee."

Bram raises his eyebrows, impressed. "How'd you manage that?"

I pull my shirt sleeve up to my shoulder and flex my rather unsubstantial bicep.

Bram coughs out a laugh. "I see."

"The RV is ready to go. I can pull it around back and then we'll get you loaded up inside. I don't know that doctors are the most plentiful these days, but we'll do our damnedest to find you one. We'll get you some help."

Bram smiles again, and I can tell that if he had a little more energy the smile would have been a full-throated laugh. "Help?

Well geez professor, that's just wonderful!" Bram's voice is raspy and wet, terminal.

"It's gonna be okay," I say, regretting the lie immediately. It's almost instinct. They're the words I've heard said to a hundred actors in a hundred movies, and I can't help repeating it now. It's an impulse, I suppose, to offer whatever comfort is available in the moment, even if the situation is as hopeless as it is now.

"What's in the bag?" he asks, noticing the satchel across my shoulder.

"Couple of knives I found in the rigs out back. A couple packs of cigarettes."

He smiles again. "You don't say?"

I return the smile. "I do say."

"Bum a smoke?"

"Bum the pack if you like."

"Let's start with one and see where it leads."

"You'll get hooked on 'em is where it'll lead. Trust me, I've been there."

"I'll take my chances, amigo."

"We have to go, Dominic," Jones commands. And then, despite Abramowitz's presence, says, "He'll die if we don't get out of here."

"I'm dead or I'm not, Jonesey. What's been done is done. And me leaving here isn't going to change that. I'll just die in the RV."

I'm touched by the compassion in Abramowitz' voice and the effort he's putting forth to keep his friend from panicking.

"There's nothing to be done about it now, Mr. Jones. There's no hospitals anymore. No medicine. And even if there is some lone doctor out there in the wilderness, we'll never find him. It's done. I'll either make it or I won't."

"Then you won't! Not just sitting here you won't."

Abramowitz smiles and shrugs. "Then I won't. So let me have my cigarette."

Jones walks away shaking his head, and I move in close to Abramowitz, tapping the top of the Winston soft pack and popping a single tube of tobacco out into my hand. I put that one between my lips and then pop out another and place it between Abramowitz's. "I'm gonna join you if that's okay, but first I need to find us some matches. I'll be right back."

"Have at it, sir."

The aisle directly outside the receiving area—aisle eleven—contains automotive and grill supplies, and within seconds I find a box of large wooden matchsticks. Beside them is a ring of automatic grill lighters, the long wand types that are filled with butane and eject a small flame at the end with the click of a button. I grab the box of matches and all four of the sealed wands, stuffing those into my satchel, feeling certain they'll come in handy at some point in the future.

There are also two flares of the variety I've just used on the roaming crab, and I load those inside as well.

On the way back to the receiving room, I push open the cardboard drawer of matches and take out a matchstick, striking it against the grainy side of the box. The flame lights instantly and I place it against the tip of my dangling Winston, inhaling as I do, lavishing in the sweet smell of the tobacco as it fills my nostrils. I stop and close my eyes for just a moment as the sweet rush of nicotine floods my head and chest. God I miss smoking.

I exhale the smoke and walk back inside the receiving area, heading directly back to the cage where Abramowitz continues to struggle. I flick another match against the box and then hold the flame near the cigarette barely clinging to his mouth.

And as the flame nears his face, he screams the shrill scream of terror.

I step back, astonished at this reaction, not quite knowing what it's in response to. "What is it? What happened? Is it the pain?"

Abramowitz doesn't answer; he only stares at the flame, eyes wide, shoulders pushing back against the metal of the carts, trying to get as far from me as possible.

"I think he's delirious," Jones says. "I think he's in shock."

Abramowitz shakes his head, shivering in fear, his mouth open wide, the cigarette now lying on the floor, the whiteness of the paper stark against the dark gray floor.

"Oh my god," Smalley says, backing away from the cages. "Oh my god, look at his leg."

Abramowitz's right pants leg, starting at a location about halfway up his shin—the place where his foot was severed from the rest of him—and ending at the lower part of his thigh, has disintegrated beneath him into the puddle of blood below. His leg underneath has turned to a solid white, matching the cigarette below.

"What is happening?" I say, rhetorically, astonished. I'm confused more than frightened at this point.

"It can't be," Jones utters. "I...It can't..."

I look up to Abramowitz's face again, and the expression across it has transformed from one of resolve and peace—peace at the certainty of his demise, I assume—to one of distress and disbelief. He takes in a labored breath and tries to lean forward, attempting to get a glimpse of what's happening below, but he doesn't have the strength to move his torso more than a few inches. "I can feel it," he says, his voice a whispery awe.

Smalley, Jones, and I back up almost in unison, as if we've just discovered that Abramowitz is the carrier of some catastrophic plague.

To this point, it hasn't occurred to me exactly what happened, about the cause of the wound. It was the crab obviously, but the means by which Abramowitz's leg was separated from his body is unknown.

"What happened?" I ask slowly, suspiciously, not focusing on either of my companions as I ask the question.

"What do you mean?" Smalley replies.

I look up at Smalley now, squinting. "I mean to his leg. How did it happen?"

"He was at the door, keeping watch. You saw him."

I nod. "And?"

"He said he turned just for a second, I guess to see if you made it out of the door or not, and then the instant you rolled out, I heard the scream. I turned and the thing had him by the shoe. It crawled up his leg like some kind of, I don't know, crab, actually. Bram scrambled away at first, I thought he was going to get away, but it got him by the ankle. And then..." Smalley swallows and takes a deep breath. "It took a giant bite right on top of his shin. It sounded like it was biting an apple." Smalley looks at Abramowitz sheepishly, seemingly embarrassed by her lack of discretion. She lowers her voice and turns her back to the dying man, whispering now. "Then it started to ravage his leg. And when Jones finally pulled him away, well, there we are."

I stay silent, not sure exactly the purpose of my questions, unclear what help the answers will be to Abramowitz now. But it's information. If it doesn't help us now, it may be useful later.

"Is that why he's turning white?" Smalley asks, again, her voice a little louder than necessary. But it is, of course, the only question.

I look back to Abramowitz and notice the white crab features—I don't pretend they're anything but that now—have moved from his right thigh and have now spread up the entire right side of Abramowitz's body. The right side of his coat and pants have turned to ash, as if chemically dissolved, like the fabric has been dipped in hydrochloric acid. Under the jacket and the layers of clothing is a naked, featureless form resembling something that used to be human.

"Holy Christ!" Jones cries, putting his hands to his mouth, his eyes massive

The white virus continues spreading, and it seems to be happening more quickly now, with each inch that overtakes the body happening faster than the last. The white infection covers Abramowitz's right shoulder and is now crawling up his neck like ice.

"Kill me," he grunts, instinctively realizing that soon his mouth will be covered, his tongue dissolved, that he won't have the chance to repeat the request. His effort to utter the words sounds immense, painful, and I have no designs on torturing him to say them again. Especially because he's right; there is nothing else to do for him now.

My first thought is to break open the package containing one of the automatic lighters, and to hold the flame near the new crab's skin, to gather more data about what happens in the presence of fire. I know that every animal has an instinctual fear of fire, but the crabs seem more fearful, almost irrationally so. The scenario to test the effects further is perfect, particularly because even if Abramowitz transforms entirely by the time I get the package open, he won't be able to do much damage with his leg severed.

I'm lost in these thoughts now, sweating the perspiration of a madman. But I can't do it. Even if it was something Abramowitz wanted, even if it was for our future survival, it would be a monstrous thing to make him suffer for my own ex-perimentation. In seconds, I discard the plan, ignoring the guilt that it leaves in its wake.

Instead, I place the duffel on the ground and reach inside, grabbing two of the Bowie knives from the rigs. I hold them both up in front of my eyes, and then quickly return the smaller one to the bag.

I walk solemnly to Abramowitz, knife in hand, trying to build up courage, to harvest the resolve I'll need to do what I must.

I nearly scream at the sight of Abramowitz now. His face is a featureless curtain of white, his eyebrows and hair are gone, as if erased from his head like a pencil drawing from construction paper. His eyes have become the tiny orbs of black that all the ghosts possess.

But unlike the former crabs, there is no fight from him. It's as if the transition has paralyzed him, similar to the way a snake shedding its skin or a lobster molting into its new shell becomes helpless during the process. He looks completely vulnerable, and I feel overwhelmed with sadness for this newly formed creature.

I hold the knife to the head of the thing that was Abramowitz only moments ago, and it looks at me, blinking its black eyes, expressionless.

"Wait," Jones says, stepping up beside me. "You shouldn't have to live with this. He's my...was my friend. I'll do it."

There's nothing to argue about, so I nod and hand Jones the knife. "I'm sorry," I say, and then walk to the threshold of the receiving room. "I'll be out front in the RV. We should get going as soon as we can. I don't know how long they'll stay gone."

Jones nods and says, "You go to, Smalley. You don't need to be here for this."

I expect Smalley to protest, to say she'll stay and see Jones through the moment, but I can see now that the fact of her leader's transition to this monster has begun to take its toll on her. There are tears in her eyes, tears that she's trying desperately to keep at bay. "Thanks, Jonesy. I'll see you in a bit."

Smalley gives a final look towards the body of Abramowitz and then walks away, rushing past me out the receiving door and into the main grocery. Before I turn to follow, I see a new energy coming from the ghost body of Abramowitz; it's begun to struggle now, its head is twisting on its neck as if trying to free itself from some invisible trap. The crab then opens its mouth and makes a sound like an angry snake, its teeth bared.

Jones closes his eyes and holds the knife to the crab's neck, steadying it by placing his hand on the top of the crab's head. "I'm sorry," I whisper again and then walk out the door.

# Chapter 9

In the light of the morning sun, the D&W hangar/warehouse looks even bigger than it did yesterday at dusk, and despite the fact that there is not a single car or truck parked in the front lot, I have a biting feeling that something is happening inside. It's not a noise, per se, but some other sense, one that I can't quite explain.

After Jones finished his duty in the back of Gray's Grocery, before we left for the night, he convinced Smalley and me to come back in and loot the store for all we could. It was a good plan, since we all three knew that no matter what, we wouldn't be coming back. We took what non-perishables we could carry, as well as several dozen pounds of chicken and fish and steak. It may not all get eaten before it spoils, but we'll give it a shot, and it doesn't do any good to turn rotten in the store. Last night we ate like lions, devouring half the steak, delicious porterhouses that Smalley cooked like a pro over the small kerosene grill.

Also, we took every source of fire that remained in the store.

"Tell me again why you think this is worthwhile," Smalley asks. We're still sitting in the RV, debating the tactics we'll use once we enter the building.

"This is the company. This is the only thing I know. And unless you two want to come entirely clean about what you know, then we should start here."

I've opened a gap for either Smalley or Jones to lay all the cards down, but neither speaks up.

"I told you, two of the people from the diner, one of whom is with the group I'm trying to find, knew this event was coming. And they worked here."

"Well, look around, Dom, there's no one here. Do you see any signs of anything?"

I keep my intuition to myself. "No, I don't, but that might be a good thing. If we can get inside, maybe we can find some clues about what happened. About *why* it happened."

"And then what?"

"I don't know, Smalley...and for Christ's sake, do we still have to talk like we're in goddamn boot camp or something? What is your name, Smalley? Your first name."

If I didn't know better, I would have thought I saw Soldier Smalley blush. She forces her eyes to stay on mine, and a trace of a smile forms at the corners of her mouth. "Stephanie."

I smile back and nod. "Stephanie's a pretty name. How about we go with that from here on out?"

She drops her gaze now and shrugs. "Fine by me."

"And how about you, Mr. Jones—if that is your real name." It's a joke, but Jones doesn't crack a grin. "What did your mother call you when you were a wee lad?"

I can see the resistance in Jones' posture, not wanting to get roped into my line of questioning. But it's quickly followed by the gestures of someone who deems it pointless to make a thing out of *not* telling me. "Stewart," he says finally, giving me an *are-you-happy-now?* look.

"Ooh, yeah, 'Stewart.' Well, how about we just stick with Jones?"

With that he laughs and then shakes his head slowly. "I don't really give a crap what you call me, but I do want to know that if we're going to risk our lives to go in this place, that we're doing it for a purpose."

"You got a bad feeling, Mr. Jones?"

"Look, I'm not expecting to live forever, or even through today, if I'm being honest, but I don't want to be stupid either." He leans forward, peering through the windshield, doing a wide scan of the building. "It looks like a daunting place to be wandering around. And yes, I do have a bad feeling. Usually do."

"I don't know any more than you do, but I think we have to do this. Even more than look for..." I pause, suddenly feeling overwhelmed by the memory of my missing group, feeling like I've betrayed friends, cost them their lives. "We'll just start at the front and work our way through the building."

"You think the place is unlocked?"

"I think the whole damn front of the place is made of glass. And I see enough rocks to build Stonehenge. That makes it unlocked."

We've double-parked the RV directly next to the building's entrance, in front of the huge doors, making sure it's as close as possible if we need to escape quickly, not wanting to make the same errors we did at the grocery store, if and when it comes time to escape.

I exit the vehicle first and walk to the front door; Stephanie and Jones follow.

The doors are locked of course, but before I simply fire a boulder through the center, I walk around the side of the building, checking if any of the emergency doors have been opened, perhaps in the blast's aftermath. They're locked as well, and I walk back to the front.

Smalley is standing with her face nearly on the glass, and she slaps a few knocks on it, and then looks over to Jones who's staring at her, bemused.

"What?" she asks, splaying her fingers. "Might as well start out polite."

"Why?"

"I'll just feel better about myself."

"I'm not sure that's going to work," I say, frowning. "I think we'll need to use a little bit more rugged method." I dip my head toward a large rock garden that buttresses against the building, lining the sidewalk of the entrance. I walk over and Smalley follows. I pick up one of a hundred meatloaf-sized rocks.

"That's not fair. Why do you get all the fun?"

"I agree. It wouldn't be fair. Have at it, Stephanie."

I get the mayhem started, walking back about ten paces and then turning back toward the building. I dip my right shoulder, allowing gravity to pull the miniature boulder low, stretching my arm fully while fingering the rock to achieve the perfect grip. I take a deep breath and then I hop forward once and step in the direction of the door, swinging my arm forward and releasing the large stone.

The rock sails through the air and catches the glass dead center, shredding that section of the pane with ease, as if it was made of a thin glaze of ice. It enters the building like a dying bird, leaving a hole in the glass almost identical to the size of the stone itself.

I see Smalley position herself now, turning left towards me, a southpaw. She takes her hop step and sends her projectile low, taking out a large section of the glass at knee level.

We both stand still, staring at the destruction, and the first thing I notice is that the sights and sounds seem out of place. This is the wrong reaction to vandalism; there's no alarm blaring or emergency lights flashing to signal the intrusion.

But those basic security systems have all been dead for weeks now. It's a new world. A world without power. I've known and accepted this reality since several weeks back, but it seems like every day there's something new to remind me.

Two more stones fly, then two more, and in less than a minute, the large door of the fancy building is disintegrated. The final throws are largely unnecessary—clearly we're done now; the entrance is gaping, wide enough that we'll barely need to turn our bodies to enter—but we threw them anyway, trying to hit any final shards we could find. It's an act of catharsis, of course, perhaps with a dusting of juvenility.

Stephanie Smalley turns and looks at me, a smile on her face, her breathing labored. "Goddamn that was fun."

I smile back. "Yes it was, Stephanie."

We both look at Jones, equal looks of sympathy on both of our faces. He can't understand what we feel at this moment, not yet, not until he finds his own outlet, his own small way to vent his frustrations over the new world he lives in. The demonstration Smalley and I just gave was small in the big scheme of things, but we both fully understand the necessity of what just took place.

With the glass now eliminated, there is a clear line of sight into the building, but there is only a blank white wall visible from the front doorway. Once we enter, however, and follow the wall about twenty yards down the hallway to the right, the whole place opens up into a massive room, more in line with the enormity of the place from the outside.

This front room looks like some kind of lobby—albeit a lobby one might find in an airport or the rotunda of a large museum—and it's austerely decorated, containing only four or five separate islands of couches and chairs evenly spaced throughout the room. Further into the lobby, across a wide expanse of nothingness, is a long, high desk that seems clearly to have been used as the reception desk during D&W's days of operation.

Behind the desk, stretching the entire width of the room, a room that can't be less than a hundred yards wide, is a metal wall that rises floor to ceiling like the gate to a medieval castle. For all the formality and refinement of the room—sterility is probably the more apt description—there is no play at keeping that image up when it comes to security. Whoever approved the design of this building was not taking any shortcuts on security, and if that meant screwing with the interior architecture, so be it.

It's also obvious that the shape of the room matches the shape of the building on the outside—Smalley, Jones, and I are standing at the beginning of a long tube, and if we could tear down the wall in front of us and look straight ahead, the building would go on forever. So it's great that we got this far into the building, but behind the metal wall, that's where the business goes down. That's where we need to get.

"Jesus Christmas," Smalley says. "This place is freaking weird. Look at that wall, man. What kind of maniac wouldn't at least put some drywall over that thing? Give it a coat of paint. I feel like I'm in a science-fiction movie."

"You are in one," I say, not even trying to be funny. "You've been in one for a couple of months now."

"Yeah, I guess that's right, but still, what kind of person makes a place like this?"

Jones nods his head as he studies the room, and then answers, as if he knows exactly what he's talking about. "The kind of person who wants everyone who enters this place to know that the only way they're getting past this room and to the meat of the building is if they're invited."

He walks forward toward the desk, continuing to study the room. Smalley and I follow.

"You coming in for a job interview?" he continues. "Got a delivery of flowers. Or pizza or Chinese or the new business cards that just finished printing? You better just plan on parking your ass in one of these chairs until you're called." He runs his hand across the back of a stiff, red chair. "No exploring allowed. Ever."

We reach the front of the desk and stop. "Well then," I say, "I guess that raises the obvious question: how are *we* supposed to get through?" I'm looking intensely at Jones. My question is sincere, challenging the man for an answer.

Jones frowns and twitches his head, never taking his eyes from the thick metal door, which looks twice as imposing from the distance we are now. He says nothing.

"There's got to be a key, right? Maybe here behind the desk or something?" I walk around the front of the desk and assume the position behind it, the position of the receptionist. I pull on the drawers that line the behemoth piece of mahogany furniture. They're locked.

Jones continues to stare at the door for a few more seconds and then turns to me, as if the question has broken him from a spell. He scoffs and shakes his head. "This isn't some Podunk restaurant on the South River. This is a billion-dollar building. Maybe several billion. This place is serious. It may not look like much from the freeway, but look at this place. And who knows what kind of technology is back there.

"Yeah, it's impressive," I agree. My voice containing a *so what?* tone.

"My point is, with a place like this, there's no key to the door. Not to that door." Jones raises his eyebrows and dips his head toward the back wall. "Not to the door that leads to the kingdom."

"So we need a badge? That's what I told Stella."

"Who's Stella again?" Smalley asks.

"Not even a badge," Jones says, not allowing us to digress. "Look at the door. There's no badge reader for that door. There's a key pad. Only a code will open that door. Probably no less than eight digits, and probably changed frequently. So unless you know what that number is—or have a thousand years to figure it out—you're not getting through."

"Why can't we just break it down?" Smalley asks. It's the question of a child, but it needed to be asked.

Jones hesitates, blinking quickly several times, processing the question, and then he busts into a full laugh.

"What?"

"Break it down? With what? More of your rocks? You think that will work?"

"No, I didn't mean with ro—"

"No!" Jones snaps, and then softens his eyes almost immediately, putting his hands up in a silent apology, shaking his head as if to strike the outburst from the record. "No, we don't have what we need to get through that door. Not even close. We need a code. Without it we'll need dynamite. Maybe. A grenade launcher, perhaps. And I'm not even sure those would work. It's over. This was a good idea, we needed to investigate this place, but it's a dead end. Let's just head to the river and see if we can find Dominic's friends. That was the original plan anyway. If we find—"

And then we hear it, a sound exploding from the middle section of the door, reverberating through the air with the tenor and danger of electricity. The sound buzzes again, and this time I theorize it's the work of some magnetic device, releasing the thick latches that secure the door. The metallic noises resonate like the pop of a pistol, inciting in me a similar level of terror.

A second later, three voices begin to ring through the cavernous room as two women and a man step out into the lobby. They're in mid-conversation, obviously not expecting to see anything resembling the mayhem that has taken place in the lobby area.

The door swings wide towards the desk, only a few steps from where I'm standing. If the door had been hinged on the other side, and opened away from the reception desk, the people exiting would have seen us instantly. Jones and Smalley sprint silently around to the far side of the desk, moving away from the door, crouching down as they turn the corner. They glide in like paratroopers and stop on a dime as they sidle up beside me. No one is making eye contact. No one is breathing.

"I don't understand why we have to come all the way out here for a bag of pretzels and a soda," one of the female voices complains. "A billion-dollar company, you'd think they would be able to afford a vending machine in more than one location."

"It has nothing to with being able to afford," the male voice instructs. "It's a security issue."

"Potato chips and candy bars?"

"Yes, actually. How would the vendor get back in the crypt to stock the machines? Can you imagine the process for something so trivial? It's too much of a hassle. The powers that be certainly aren't going to allow it just so as not to inconvenience low-level employees like you two."

"Listen to you now," the other woman says. "Gets a promotion and suddenly he's no longer a member of the same class."

"Damn right."

"You and Colonel Badass and Ms. Wyeth are—"

"What the f...?"

I can hear the awe in the voice of the first woman as she cuts off her profanity mid-word, and I know instantly it's her reaction to the shattered front windows. These three employees—I can't know their positions at this point, but there seems to be a level of hierarchy separating the man from the women—obviously didn't hear the shattering from behind the thick steel door; but they sure as hell can see the damage now, the entire first story of the building's glass front has detonated across the floor of the lobby.

"What?" the other woman asks. "What is it?" And then, almost immediately, she cries, "Oh my god!"

"Who's here?" the male voice shouts, his voice suddenly masculine and alert. I can almost see his head on a swivel, whipping his eyes around the room, searching for the danger.

I've yet to take a breath, my eyes wide, animated, trying to catch the looks of my companions, both of whom have maneuvered themselves in front of me now, facing me. But their eyes are still averted, up and to the side, listening.

"Maybe it's just vandals, Spence? You think? Maybe they just busted the door and left."

"It's not vandals. Anyone still in the cordon who took the time to do this would have ripped the place apart. Look at the furniture. It's all untouched."

I can hear the man—Spence—take a step in our direction, toward the desk, the tight rubber soles of his shoes clicking out past the doorway and around to the front of the reception area.

Jones still doesn't meet my stare, despite the telepathic shouts I'm hurling in his direction, and instead presses two fingers on top of Smalley's forearm. She snaps her head towards him, meeting his gaze, and Jones tips his head in the direction of the door, pauses for a moment, and then nods back to her. He then touches his chest and dips his chin in the direction of the clicking heels.

Smalley blinks a couple times and then nods, a gesture that says she's deciphered the charade and is ready to go. Her face is serious, focused, and for the first time since our original encounter at the Clam Bake, I see the soldier in her.

Finally, I wave a hand low, and get their attention, and I flip up my hands. *What about me?* But Jones only holds up a hand and shakes me off, and then points to the floor, telling me to stay put.

I'm offended at first by the snub, particularly after the heroic acts I performed inside the grocery store and at the gift store of the Clam Bake. I can hold my own. If it wasn't for me, in fact, we'd all be dead now, massacred by the horde at the entrance of Gray's Grocery.

But that's a pointless position for me to take now. It's not a contest to see who's been a bigger badass, it's about continuing to survive. And Jones and Smalley seem better suited to lead that endeavor at the moment. I can feel the calmness coming from them both. They seem to be in their environment, hunkered down in wait while the enemy paces around us, silently sending codes to one another, having already formed a plan before I've even been acknowledged.

I mouth the word "Okay," and then Jones puts his hand against my right hip and presses, moving me to the side, out of the way. He crouches forward, taking my place under the desk, and then holds up three fingers above his head, making sure to keep it below the height of the desk. I look back and see that Smalley is fixed on his fingers.

"What are we going to do, Spence? Maybe we should call in the airlift. They'll want us to do that. We have to go tell them. Maybe they can get us out of here today instead. I mean they'll want to leave, right? If someone is here, inside—if they're inside—we have to get out."

"Stop talking!" Spence snaps. The voice is right in front of us, just on the other side of the desk, slightly past where the three of us are stooped, hidden.

I look back to Jones, his three fingers still frozen above him. And then the three fingers become two. Then one.

When the last finger falls and the hand becomes a closed fist, Smalley, still crouched, takes two steps toward the edge of the desk that's closest to the interior steel door where the three D&W workers emerged. And then she rises up.

Simultaneously, Jones explodes to his feet, almost causing me to shriek at the force of the motion. There's not a single muscle twitch wasted in the movement, and within seconds, the man called Spence, recently promoted by D&W upper-management, is lying flat on his back atop the reception desk. Jones is hovering above him, his arm wrapped tightly around his neck.

Concurrent with Jones' attack, I hear the shrieks of the two women, presumably from the sight of Smalley appearing in a dash from behind the desk. But the two shrieks become one almost instantly, as the first scream is replaced by the sound of colliding bodies.

There's too much happening for me to stay put, and against Jones' command, I follow Smalley's path from behind the desk. I clear the view of the desk and can now see the result of the collision sound. One of the women is lying on the ground about six feet from Smalley, and Smalley has wedged her body between the steel door and the jamb.

The second woman is standing about ten feet away from the door and is backing up slowly toward the front entrance, rotating her look between Jones, Smalley, and now me.

"Who the fuck are you?" Spence asks, the crook of Jones' arm around his neck severely limiting the clarity of his voice.

Jones ignores the question. "Dominic, get behind her. Don't let her leave."

I quickly run past the startled woman and position myself between her and the open glass façade. But it seems unnecessary at the moment. The woman is stunned, and she gives no indication that she plans to flee.

"She's not going anywhere," Spence says. "Where is she going to go? She wouldn't make it three hours out there."

"We have to get back inside," the woman on the floor says, her voice teetering on panic, now recognizing their vulnerability. "We're not secure anymore. We can't stay here."

"Who are you," Spence repeats. "What are you doing here? This is a private, legal business. You have no right to be here." He squirms, kicking his feet out, testing Jones' grip. But the soldier squeezes tighter, gagging the man, locking him down tighter in the bend of his elbow, using it like the jaws of a vise.

Spence tries to speak again, and this time, Jones pulls him fully over the top of the desk and down to the floor. They both disappear from view, and for a moment, all we can hear are the violent sounds of a scuffle.

In a matter of moments, Jones rises back to his feet, and then a second later, he raises his clenched fist and brings Spence up in front of him by the back collar of his shirt. There's a small pistol in Jones' hand now; the barrel of it is slanted up in the direction of Spence's skull.

"Wasn't expecting this prize at the end?" Jones says. "It's a good thing too, because I probably would have gone with a different strategy."

Jones looks over at Smalley for the first time since the plan unfolded and smiles weakly. "Thank god. You got there in time. Something tells me Mr. Spencer here would have died before giving us the code."

"Damn right I would." Spence replies, and there's nothing in his tone to suggest he's lying.

"Please don't hurt us." It's the woman who Smalley shoved to the floor. She's now on her feet, holding her left arm at the bicep. "We didn't have anything to do with...whatever happened. We just work here. It was—"

"Shut up, Pam," Spence interrupts, but the command lacks energy and authority.

"You didn't have anything to do with what?" I ask.

Pam averts her eyes from Spence. "What happened here. The experiment."

"Shut up!"

"They know, Spence. They're here. They wouldn't be here if they didn't know."

"What else?" Jones asks. "How far does it go? Is it everywhere? Is it the world?"

"God no," the woman answers. Her voice is a whisper. "The world?"

I can see the genuine confusion in the woman's eyes, the disbelief that we're that out of touch with what's happening.

"Why would you think that? Is that what they told you?"

It is what they told us, of course. The early radio broadcasts said the world was a frozen ball of ice now. But it was obviously just part of it, part of the whole plan to keep us contained. Stella, Tom, Danielle and I had floated that theory, that it was part of the experiment, and now I know it's true. Thank God. There's hope.

I think of my other group again, whom I'm now certain are dead, but I shake the thought away, trying to stay focused.

"How are you alive?" the other woman, the one I'm guarding from leaving, asks. "How could you be alive still living out there? They're everywhere now."

"How do you know that?" Smalley asks. "How do you know what's out there? I thought you couldn't survive for three hours out there. How do you know what's happening then?"

She shakes her head, bewildered by the question. "I see them when we leave the cordon. We all see them."

"You leave?"

Again, a head shake of puzzlement. "Of course we leave? Did you think we lived here?"

"Goddamn it, Sydney," Spence says, the words spitting out through tightly gritted teeth. He's apparently re-energized and resuming his authority over the women. "If you say another fucking word, I will—"

"You're not gonna do a goddamn thing!" Smalley interrupts, pointing a finger of warning at Spence, who, with the muzzle of a pistol currently resting against his head, is in no position to argue.

"*How* do you leave?" Smalley asks calmly. "I don't see any cars out there. You have some kind of limo service that comes and picks you up?"

"The airlift," Jones says. "She mentioned an airlift a minute ago. They must have a helicopter come in. Is that it?"

The woman nods. "Yes."

"Christ," I say. "So how does that work exactly? You have a landing pad on the roof?"

"No. Inside."

"Inside? Inside the building? You mean the roof opens up?"

The woman nods again.

"Jesus, who the hell owns this place?"

"Nameless and faceless, that's who. Like I said, we just work here. You have to believe us, we had no idea what was going on with the experiment. Not really."

"I'm getting very tired of hearing that."

"So the airlift isn't coming today. When's the next one?"

"It's supposed to be Wednesday," Pam answers. "But sometimes they come a day early, sometimes a day late."

I look at Jones and Smalley, and I can tell instantly they're having the same confused reaction that I am. "What day is today?" I ask.

Pam frowns and looks away, embarrassed, ashamed at the suffering that she, if not the direct cause of, has at least played some role in administering. "Tuesday," she says.

"Looks like we have some time to kill then," Smalley says, and then clicks her head up toward the front entrance of the building. "And we certainly can't hang around here. Check it."

I turn around slowly, and in the fraction of a second it takes for my vision to span the vast expanse of the lobby toward the building's front door, two crabs have crawled through the gaping holes where two glass doors used to be. The bloody streaks left by the shards of glass are already apparent on their heads and torsos, even from this distance, so stark white are their bodies.

Two more crabs climb up behind the first two, entering with the same careless aggression, slowly but unceasing in their advancement.

"Oh my god!" Sydney yells. "Oh my god, it's them." This sentence starts as a murmur, and then it crescendos with each word that follows. "They're inside. We have to shoot them!"

Jones frowns and keeps the gun pointed at Spence, but I can see a hint of concern steadily growing on his face. "They're too far away. It would be a waste of ammo."

"As I was saying," Smalley chimes in, "maybe now would be a good time to go have a look around." She throws a look over her shoulder. "Back there."

I agree and begin walking back to the interior door where Smalley stands ready to go. I corral Sydney on the way, forcing her to move with me. Pam needs no motivation to go in the same direction and is already next to Smalley, waiting for the rest of us.

"Let's go," Jones says, walking Spence from around the reception desk, his hand still gripped tightly on the back collar of the man's shirt. They take the wide route to get to the door, exiting the confines of the reception desk on the side opposite where the interior door is located and walking around to the front. As they reach the midsection of the desk, about halfway to the door, Spence thrusts his shoulders forward and bucks his head like a horse, and in less than half a second, he has easily broken free of Jones' grasp and is making a run for it, away from us and toward the oncoming crabs.

"Hey!" Jones calls, and then takes a few instinctive steps in pursuit. But after three or four paces he stops abruptly, seeming to grasp the inanity of chasing.

"Spence, no!" Pam commands. "What are you doing?" The last cry is that of a lover. Or perhaps of someone who wishes to be. I study her face as I approach the door, her age and features, and the match with Spence suddenly makes sense.

Spence stops a little past the halfway point between us and the front entrance, which is just about far enough away that he no longer fears being shot. He then turns back, staring, first at Pam, and then at Jones. The crabs are still thirty yards or so away from him and, at the moment, still plodding forward, not quite attacking.

"We're not going to hurt you, Spence," I call. "We just wanted answers. That's why we're here. The people here have destroyed a lot of lives, mine included. We just want to know what happened. Why it happened. And how to leave this place and get back to life."

Spence bows his head and puts his hand at the back of his neck. It's a movement that signals both guilt and exhaustion. He lifts his head and stares at me. "I know. I know that's what you want. And I can't give it to you. Not the answers and not the escape plan."

"Who then?"

"It doesn't matter. I can't stay. If I'm here when she finds out what happened, she'll have me killed. One of them will."

"Killed?"

Spence shrugs. "It's my job to keep this place secure. To keep any internals out. The breach of the lobby is one thing, that's not entirely within my control. But the labs, that's something else."

Spence seems to be making an indirect plea for us to let the door close, to spare him the consequences that will come from allowing us to get inside. But that will never happen. We're entering the lab area whether it means his death or not.

"Who are you talking about?" I ask. "If you're leaving anyway, then just tell us." But Spence has said his peace. He turns and looks back to the crabs again, measuring their distance from him, calculating how long he has until he makes his ultimate getaway. He's got another minute or two it seems; the white ghosts continue their desultory throng of the lobby, unconcerned with the unfolding of our drama. But I've seen it several times now—the escalation to madness can happen in an instant.

I look from Spence to Pam and repeat my question. "Who is he talking about?"

"Mrs. Wyeth," Pam says.

"Who is that?"

"She's the supervising manager of the lab—kind of like the CEO of this place. She's been gone since the blast. Everyone thought she was dead. Everyone thought she got caught up in the blast."

"And you kept working anyway? You kept coming in?"

"We kept getting orders. The airlifts in and out continued. Companies don't stop operating just because the boss dies."

It's not an exact analogy, but I let it go. "Who gives these orders?"

"The colonel. And others. People above him, I guess."

"Nameless and Faceless?" I ask.

"Exactly."

"And now she's here? This Wyeth woman? Where was she all this time?"

"We still don't know. She just showed up yesterday. Walked in like it was a typical weekday morning, coffee in hand, barking orders."

"Spence said she would kill him. Is that true?"

"I don't know anything about that. I don't know why he said that. The people who run this place are pretty uptight, military types, but I've never seen or heard anyone being treated inhumanely" Pam's voice is nervous now, like she's about ready for the conversation to end as well.

"No? What about the thousands of people that were turned into monsters by this company? And then were prevented from leaving by armies at the borders. Does any of that count as inhumane?"

"Leave her alone," Sydney says quietly, uneasily. "She didn't do anything?"

"What kind of company is this? What kind of company produces weapons that kill innocent people? And whose management kills people that don't do their job?"

"Welcome to D&W," Sydney says with a nervous laugh, and then immediately begins to cry.

I look back to the entrance of the D&W building and watch as Spence begins his run to freedom. He takes a wide berth, nearly brushing up against the far wall of the lobby, and then sprints toward the shattered opening of the glass doorway. He steers clear of the crabs, passing them like he's returning a punt in a college bowl game as he goes, dodging each of them easily before reaching the passage and exiting through the empty frame. Some of the white ghosts give a passive look as he flees, but they make no move to catch him. They're halfway through the lobby now and advancing.

I look back to Pam, whom I've decided is the more knowledgeable of the two women, the more experienced worker at

D&W. "So what, you make chemicals here? Is that it? Is that what changed normal people into that?"

Pam closes her eyes and cups her hands around her mouth, sliding them down her chin and joining them in a praying position. "Look, we don't work on the chemical side of things. Sydney and I are IT; we just keep the computers running. I've been here four years and Sydney was brought on a little over a year ago. We started hiring to prepare for some big event, and Syd and I were kept on as the emergency staff. Triple pay."

I can see that Pam regrets stating the last part of her bio, as it lumps her in with the leaders that caused this. Greed, always the motivator. She bows her head and sighs. "Anyway, yeah."

"What about Spence?" I ask.

"He's the...was the floor manager. But I swear to god, we didn't know what was coming. We didn't know about the snow and the...destruction."

"Yeah, sure."

"I swear. We knew as much as we needed to keep the systems going, and we saw things we probably shouldn't have—of course, but that's the nature of the job. But we're not like the doctors here. The scientists. They're..." Pam's voice cracks and she shakes off the rest of her sentence.

"I would advise that you not let yourselves off the hook that easily. You are a part of this. You are responsible. Keeping the computers up keeps the process going. And that does contribute to the destruction. You said you saw things, and you've already admitted that you know about the monstrosity that occurred out there. While you've been seeing these things from your comfortable charter flights in and out of hell for the past few months, we've been living it." My voice is as close to yelling as possible without actually being classified as such.

Pam and Sydney both look away, Sydney to the ground in shame, Pam to the sky, rolling her eyes in denial. "You don't—"

"I don't care!" This time I'm yelling, and I feel the desire to rush toward this woman and grab her neck with my hands, my thumbs pressing against her windpipe.

But the truth is, it's not her fault. And I know as well as anyone how easy it is to gradually get sucked into something illicit, even abominable, and then to justify each day that passes, telling yourself again and again how it isn't your fault, and, in this case, how you're just trying to make a living and provide for your family. I don't know Pam's situation; maybe triple pay buys medicine that keeps her kid alive.

"I'm sorry," Sydney says, now bawling like a child. Pam is crying too, and I can see the apology all over her face.

"What do you think fellas?" Smalley asks. You think that's close enough?" Smalley motions in the direction of the approaching crabs, several of whom are almost three quarters of the way across the lobby. They're still far enough away that we would make it through the door, but the margin of error is getting awfully thin. At any moment, one of them could get the trigger and decide to attack, and as I now know, the rest would likely follow.

"I think that's right, Stephanie. Let's go."

Jones and I follow Pam and Sydney into the back of D&W laboratories, each of us brushing past Smalley who holds the door and then falls in behind us. But just before she allows the heavy door to close behind us, to seal us in like some destructive ancient god being banished back to his tomb, I look back to watch a dozen more crabs crawling in through the broken entrance of the building, their bodies woven together to look like one big mass of flesh.

And in that last instant, one of the early approachers breaks out from the crowd and begins to run full speed toward us, and they all begin to follow.

Pam turns back and enters a code into the door; not that it matters, I think, since the crabs still don't seem to have figured out that particular skill. But still, the sound of the firing locks gives me a sense of immediate comfort. How we'll ever leave this place, I can't imagine at the moment, but that's a problem for later.

We take two or three steps inside the pre-entrance to the main laboratory, and then the dull crash of the door finalizes our position.

"Guess you picked a good time to go, Smalley," Jones says, motioning back to the closed door, where no doubt the crabs are now piling up against it.

"Just stick with me, Stewart, you'll be okay."

"There's one more thing I haven't told you," Pam says suddenly, instantly destroying the flash of light-heartedness that existed.

"Yeah, what's that?" Smalley asks.

"You remember Spence said his job was to keep internals out?"

"Yeah. What did that mean?"

"Internals. It's the name they had for anyone inside the cordon who was still living—and hadn't changed—after the blast."

"So us then," I say.

Pam nods.

"What about it? What didn't you tell us?"

"Mrs. Wyeth, when she came back..." Pam stalls, as if re-thinking her decision to tell us her secret.

"What is it, Pam?" I say, harnessing my professor voice, low and leading, like I'm trying to extract a shy student's interpretation of Goethe.

"When she came back yesterday, there were a couple of internals with her."

# Chapter 10

The hallway behind the heavy steel door is long and straight, with flat white walls on either side, cutting off about two thirds of the width of the hangar. It looks like a hallway you would expect to find in a mental institution, the kind that in movies have small-windowed doors staggered every twenty paces or so, and behind each of those, straight-jacket-bound patients screaming nonsensically as the doctors pass.

But there are no side doors in this hallway, only one directly ahead, at the end of this corridor that seems to extend forever. It looks like we're heading to some laboratory version of the gates of heaven.

There aren't doors along the wide hallway, but there are several golf carts littered about, their purpose obvious.

"I'm guessing those aren't functioning at the moment?" I ask aloud, almost rhetorically.

"No," Pam says, frowning as she shakes her head. "The supply copters bring fuel for the generators regularly, but they don't want us using the power for luxuries like golf carts." Pam uses her ring fingers and pinkies to make air quotes on the word 'luxuries,' and I almost laugh aloud at the gesture. I make an absent note to myself to steal the move if I ever get out of here.

"So you have electricity then?"

"Yeah, of course," Sydney says, "how else would the doctors, or any of us, be able to work? And how would they have kept them alive?"

"Who?" It's Smalley, and her voice lacks all remnants of playfulness.

Pam and Sydney exchange looks, and I can see a quiet acceptance between them, an understanding that all of this is about to collapse so holding back now is senseless.

"Them," Sydney says matter-of-factly, and then gives a shrug. "The changed."

"That's a pretty euphemistic term," I say. "You make it sound like these people had a bad reaction to Botox or something."

"It's what we call them. It's what they are."

"You have some of them here then?" Jones asks, his question the more obvious one, the important one at the moment."

Pam nods, "Oh yes. Nineteen of them now."

"Nineteen? Why that number?"

"There were close to fifty when we started."

We're only a few steps from the end of the corridor now and the interior door which no doubt leads to the business section of our adventure. But I'm not quite ready for the showdown. There's a chance—a good chance—that none of us makes it out of this building, and I want to know as much as I can about what happened. "So the rest of them, they were killed during experiments or something?"

"Something like that?"

"You seem to know a bit more than you let on originally, Ms. Pam," Smalley adds. I was thinking the same thing.

"I know that it happened—the blast and the people changing afterwards—and I know about that experiments were done after. And are still being done."

"Like Ms. Smalley said, that's quite a bit more."

"But I don't know why. I'm IT, I told you. Sydney and I offer tech support. But there are only a few of us still here now and...I guess things have gotten a little cozy. People get a little more comfortable with their secrets."

"But not about what the purpose of all this was? I find that hard to believe."

"It was just Spence and a few of the other doctors who kept coming here, even after Ms. Wyeth disappeared, and they didn't ask questions. I think they believed if they never heard directly why it happened, that somehow they would be exonerated of guilt. Just taking orders, I guess."

"So like Nazis then?"

"Like I said, there are people much higher than Spence and the doctors, or even Ms. Wyeth. I'm sure she knew more, but not Spence. He was just kept on to manage this place: coordinate the copters, order supplies, that kind of thing. Make sure the trains ran on time. But they never told him about any of the reasons."

"How can you know that? For sure?"

Pam's eyes soften, and I can see in them the pain from earlier, during Spence's escape, and it's obvious now that a fair bit of pillow talk took place between the two of them. "I know."

We finally reach the door at the end of the corridor, and, like the interior lobby door, it too has a keypad on the wall to the right of it.

"I'm assuming you know the code, Pam?" I say, the exhaustion in my voice unmistakable, even to my own ears. "Because this would have been a whole lot of work for nothing."

"I do."

I look over to Jones and Smalley and then back to Pam. "Let's do it then. Let's find this Wyeth lady."

"I need you to put the gun to my head," she replies, no trace of humor on her face, no hesitation in her voice.

"What?" Jones asks.

"Listen, like you, I don't know how any of this is going to end up. But if it ends with the three of you dying, I don't want us to be seen as accomplices to your infiltration. I'll help you as much as I can—we both will—we understand that what happened in this county is horrible and illegal—a cataclysm—and the people responsible for it deserve to be punished. Severely. Maybe they even deserve to die." Pam dips her head for a moment in thought and then looks up again. "Yes, they do deserve to die. But you also don't know these people. You've seen what they were willing to do just to create this...I don't know, weapon, I guess?"

The word 'weapon' smashes against the inside of my brain, and I know now that there could be no other purpose for the creation of the crabs.

"So if they're willing to do that, what do you think they'll do to protect themselves from going to prison? Or getting a lethal injection?"

Jones speaks up, tipped off by some other portion of Pam's explanation for her request. "Who exactly is back here? You said doctors and a woman—and the white monsters, which I assume are locked up somewhere. Is there someone else we should be aware of?'

Pam looks down again and over at Sydney, whose eyes are wide, riveted on her co-worker, trusting in whatever she decides to do.

"There are three soldiers. Armed obviously. Military-grade rifles. And then the Colonel and Mrs. Wyeth."

"And the ghosts—the Changed—I'm right to assume they're caged?"

"Most of them are in a large open room at the back of the arena, with glass paneling all around. Think of a hockey rink, except instead of ice, the floor is covered with snow."

"Arena?" I ask.

"That's what we call the main section of this building, just on the other side of this door. The building is a converted hangar, and like a hangar, it's all very open. And they didn't build any lower ceilings when they renovated it, so it kind of feels like you're in a stadium or arena."

"What kind of office building is wide open? Aren't there offices?"

"Yes, you'll see. They put up all these privacy walls to create offices and...other types of rooms, so once you walk through the main area, there are a bunch of separate rooms all lined up leading to the back where they keep the changed. It's laid out kind of like a shopping mall, the holding room at the back is the food court, I guess. But with the ceilings as high as they are, the place feels like you're in a cavern."

"What's the point? What are they doing with them?"

"Who?"

"The ghosts...crabs, changed, whatever."

Pam shrugs and frowns, as if the answer is so obvious as to be unexciting. "Studying them. Trying to figure out exactly what they created. And—I can't know this for sure—but I think they're trying to learn how to train them."

Smalley scoffs and shakes her head. "Jesus."

"And these internals you mentioned," I say, "the people from the outside, who are they?"

"I don't know." Pam shakes her head feverishly, as if remembering again that there are, in fact, new visitors to their building, other than the three of us. "I barely saw them when they came in. They were with the colonel and Ms. Wyeth and one of the soldiers, and they took them away to one of the rooms."

"How many were there?"

"I saw two. Both men. Looked like maybe a father and son. Grandfather maybe." I have no further questions at the moment, and Pam recognizes the lull and steps to the keypad, preparing to gain us entry. And then she pauses, folding her hands properly down in front of her. "I won't do this without the promise. I won't punch in this code unless you promise that, if and when we're seen, you'll stage this so that Sydney and I look like your prisoners."

Jones puts his hands up, a signal that says what other choice do I have? "Okay, I agree to that."

Pam takes a deep breath and nods, confirming the deal.

"But you need to give us a chance in there. I need to know more about the layout. I need to know where the soldiers are."

Pam nods again. "They always keep two soldiers on the roof, at the far end of the building by the landing area. They're mainly looking for any approaching hordes. The other soldier patrols the perimeter of the building, so, lucky for you, he must have been at the opposite end of the entrance when you showed up."

"Why didn't they notice us when we drove up?" Jones asked. "Or when the ghosts showed up in the lobby?"

I don't know, but I can tell you there isn't much action around here—or at least there hasn't been lately."

"Why is that?"

"They've been trying to cordon them off in different sections of the county. Trying to block them off so they can't just roam free. I think they realize they'll eventually get out, so they've been corralling them in bridges and barns and any large structures they can find."

"And they're succeeding in that?" Jones asks, "Is that what you're telling us?"

"I don't know what goes on out there, not really, other than what we see from the air. But I do know the soldiers guarding the building haven't had much to do. I catch the one on the perimeter at least once a week planted somewhere on the side of the building smoking—and not always cigarettes—and who knows what's going on up on the roof. They could be sleeping for all I know. But the perimeter guard, he'll be making his way around to the front at some point. And he'll see the..."

"What is it?"

"I was just thinking about what you said, how they were coming through the door of the lobby just when we were entering the corridor here."

"Yeah, so?"

"Terrence probably did get to the front. He probably ran smack into them."

"Oh my God." Sydney whispers, now understanding Pam's point.

The soldier—Terrence—whose job it was to secure the ground perimeter of the building, likely walked right into the oncoming horde of crabs as he was making his typical, uneventful laps around the perimeter of the D&W building. It was a place largely untouched by the virus of the white ghosts. Until now. Until we showed up. Maybe it was the sight of our

RV that brought them; perhaps they were scouting us from the woods of Gray's Grocery, and then followed us along the interstate. Or, more likely, it was the noise of the crashing windows that drew them.

"Terrence is dead, isn't he?" Sydney asks, and I quickly make another romantic connection, this time between Sydney and the guard.

Despite the potential tragedy, I have no urge to console Sydney. The truth is, I'm grateful to have one less soldier to deal with. And if the other two guards on the roof are as inept as old boy Terrence, maybe soldiers won't be an issue at all.

"We're doing a lot of speculating," Smalley says, trying to restore some faith. "We don't know anything about what happened, and there's nothing to do about it now anyway. Maybe Terrence and Spence met up and are on their way to Cabo."

No one laughs at Smalley's attempt at levity. Pam simply turns to the keypad and lifts the Lucite cover protecting the device.

For just a moment, I feel a bit sorry for Pam and Sydney, knowing that two people they've come to know over these past several weeks, whom they've formed some kind of bond, are now likely dead. Just as the members of my group likely are. Tom and Stella. Danielle and James.

With the thoughts of my friends—as well as my dead wife and mistress—my sympathy for them fades quickly, and in its place, a new stoicism sets in, a new disgust at what has occurred inside this giant, wicked palace. Pam and Sydney and Spence and Terrence, and everyone that works here, are, at least in part, culpable for the destruction of Warren County and beyond. "One more thing," I say.

Pam turns and meets my eyes, saying nothing.

"I need to know where Ms. Wyeth will be."

# Chapter 11

The deadbolt fires through the locking mechanism and un-
latches the door with a bang. As Pam pushes the door wide, I
expect to see a phalanx of soldiers standing in a line, waiting for
our arrival, rifles raised and aimed at our heads, the little laser
sights quivering ever so slightly in the middle of our chests.

Instead, beyond the door, there is only the enormous room
Pam described, though perhaps undersold a bit, and the smell
of chlorine. In another life, the smell would have reminded me
of an indoor pool, or perhaps a freshly cleaned floor, but now
it only reminds me of Sharon.

The size of this new area is at least as large as an airport terminal, except instead of the bustle and brightness of an airport,
the place is dark and empty, as if the terminal had been abandoned fifty years earlier.

This section of the D&W building mimics the expanse of
the lobby area, except instead of the thin carpeting and mini-
malist decorations of the lobby, which was at least an attempt
to make the room look civilized, here there is only cold, concrete flooring below us, above us an endless pattern of exposed
girders. The space is breathtaking in its vastness, and the lighting is so dim that I can't see all the way to either of the walls
that border us on the sides. For all I know, there are two, symmetrical lines of armed guards along the perimeter, watching us
at this moment, baiting us into some chemical trap.

But for all the darkness beside us, forward it only extends
for the first fifty yards or so. Beyond the empty stretch of space
in front, I can see the dividing walls of the offices, as well as the

reflection of light from the glass windows. These are obviously the makeshift rooms that Pam spoke of earlier.

There is no second story space in the hangar, at least none that I can see from here, but spanning the front of the first set of offices, running from side to side above the height of the open ceilings, there is scaffolding which forms a metal walkway. On either side of the scaffolding are ladders leading up to the walkway.

"Jesus, this place is big," Smalley says, understating the obvious as she seems predisposed to do. "And open. We're sitting ducks out here."

"Let's get going then," Jones says. "The back office past the hockey rink, right? That's where the boss is?"

"That's where her office is," Pam corrects. "She just got here yesterday—for the first time since the blast—so I don't know what she's up to or where she is at the moment."

"Where was she when you and Spence came out for your Fritos break?"

Pam hesitates. "With the colonel."

"And where might he be at the moment?"

"When I left they were in the observation pen. We call it the penalty box.

"Keeping with the hockey theme?" I ask.

She shrugs. "I guess."

"And what goes on in the penalty box?" Jones continues.

"It's a way for the scientists to get close to them—the changed—without risking their lives or having to walk around the outside of the holding pen."

"Do you think we could get moving?" Smalley says. "I'm starting to feel a little aquaphobic."

"Aquaphobic," Jones replies. "You scared of the ocean? I think you mean agoraphobic. And yeah, I'm with you."

Pam nods toward the offices. "It's straight ahead, toward those lights, at the end of the corridor that runs between those rows of rooms."

We begin walking in that direction, Pam sticking close to Jones, making sure she's near enough that should we be caught off guard by the security forces in this place, she and Jones will still be able to pull off the hostage charade.

When we reach the middle of the open space, I begin to feel like a character in a fantasy novel, sneaking into the lair of some sleeping dragon, just me and my trusty sidekicks, keeping a close huddle the entire time, heads on swivels, each watching his side for danger.

It feels like an eternity, but we finally reach the first of the offices, and I can see that the construction of the rooms is a little more impressive than I'd originally thought. From a distance, I had assumed the offices were shoddily made, thrown up with little more care than what's given to the erection of a lean-to. But now, standing beside the divider wall of the first room, touching it with my fingers, I can feel that it's sturdy, solid, made with purpose, each wall ten to twelve feet high with thick fiberglass windows fronting them and steel molding reinforcing the glass at every junction.

We pass the first room slowly, staring inside hypnotically, like we're walking through an aquarium. But there's nothing much to see; it looks to be a typical office. The room is dark, but there's enough ambient lighting coming from further down the hangar that we can see a standard desk and a couple of office chairs, as well as a small sofa arranged along the left side of the room. The wiring systems for a phone and a computer snake across the desk and onto the floor, though the hardware itself is no longer there.

We turn to the office on the opposite side of the corridor and it appears to be a mirror image of the one on the right. Still, it seems odd and out of place, staged maybe, an office-building version of a Potemkin village.

We walk past eight more rooms, four on each side of the main walkway that splits the offices, and they all look almost identical to the first two.

And then we reach the sixth office on the right, about halfway down the corridor to the light at the back of the arena. And things inside are very different.

"What the hell is that?" Jones whispers.

Sydney just shakes her head and swallows, blinking several times, like a child lying in bed, pretending not to hear the thunder rumbling outside her window.

"We don't look at it," Pam says. Her voice is calm, matter-of-fact, like she and Sydney have thought a lot about this particular room and have made the sensible choice to ignore it, the way you would simply ignore a dirty piece of graffiti painted on a subway train.

"But what is it?" I repeat, and then I step close to the long window that stretches from the floor to the top of the ceiling-less room.

And then I see it clearly. At the back of the office, hunched in the darkest corner of the room, facing away from us, is a crab. But it looks thinner than the others, discolored and deformed, its bony gray spine bulging against the skin of its back like the edges of a mutated pie crust.

"It's one of them," Pam says, her voice directed away from me, not giving her eyes the opportunity to drift anywhere near the room.

"What's wrong—"

With the speed of a greyhound—and nearly the build and color of one, as well—the crab scurries from the corner of the office and races towards the place where I'm standing. Its eyes are thin and focused, its teeth bared like a crazed baboon. It doesn't growl, per se, but its heavy nasal breathing is somehow a more terrifying noise.

I'm frozen, unable even to exhale as I stand inches from the glass, watching the horrible thing approach. So instead of fighting the terror, I take in the vision with fascination, the way one would if a tiger shark were approaching the side wall of its tank, feeling that primal instinct of fear but knowing the shark is no real threat. The truth is, of course, I don't really know that I'm safe in this particular environment, and unlike the shark, or any of the other crabs I've encountered to this point—save those at Gray's Grocery, perhaps—this creature doesn't have the detachment of feeling in its attack. The beast rushing at me now is deranged, angry, filled with hate.

The crab never lifts its torso more than two or three feet from the floor as it comes at me, seeming to maximize its speed by using this posture, and there is no deceleration as it crashes against the inside of the acrylic glass window, causing the entire row of offices to shake violently.

Sydney screams, and with that alarm now sounded, I have no doubt that we'll be shot within the next few seconds. But I still can't move, and I watch the dull white ghost attack me through the glass over and over again.

"Dammit, shut her up!" Jones barks at no one in particular. "She'll get us killed."

"It's okay," Pam assures, "if they're in the penalty box, they'll have a tough time hearing us. It's not completely sealed, but it's surrounded on the sides by thick glass, a lot like these offices."

"But they might not be in there now," Jones reminds her.

"Then it's too late, Jones," I say, turning slightly, trying to extricate myself from the maniacal draw of the monster behind the glass to take over for Pam in her side of the conversation. "We have to hope they are and not waste any more time. Let's keep walking."

"Hold on," Smalley scoffs, an ironic smile on her face. "What the hell is going on here? What is that thing?"

"Smalley, we have to—"

"No!" Smalley barks at me, and I can see she's almost in tears, on the verge of a breakdown, perhaps. "Why is that thing in there like that? And what's wrong with it? It looks...just wrong."

Pam looks down, assuming her earlier posture of shame. "He's one of the tests. One of the guinea pigs, I think. For the next...batch of them."

"What are you talking about?" I ask, turning completely toward Pam. My back is now facing the crab as it continues to press its hungry face against the barrier, gnashing its teeth against the impenetrable acrylic.

"Why do you think we're still here? Why would this place still be open?"

I open my mouth to speak, but nothing comes out.

"It's not over. They're not going to stop now. They've killed thousands of people." Pam looks away and swallows, and then a nervous chuckle exits her mouth, as if she's just now realizing the magnitude of what they've done here. "Why would—"

A banging sound rattles from somewhere in the back of the arena, and everyone stops in place, their stares fixed to some invisible place in space, searching for the sound with their eyes. There's silence for a beat, and then the faintest sound of a voice drifts in from the same direction as the banging.

"What the hell is that?" I ask.

Pam shakes her head. "I don't know." The answer comes a little too quickly, too assuredly.

"Come on. Let's find it."

We continue down the corridor toward the rink, leaving the white monster in a rage against the clear wall of his cell. I look back at it, and his eyes are following us as we leave, and suddenly a new fear enters my mind, that this is one of the new rulers of the world. It's too late, they've been created, and by all accounts, these mad doctors are trying to make more of them. And even if we stop them, the people who are building these demons now, what difference will it make? The technology is out there; it's probably been distributed through electronic means and is now floating around in cyberspace like some unstoppable virus.

As we progress further down the corridor, the crab fades from sight, but the banging grows steadily louder. By the time we reach the end of the rows of offices, however, the banging has stopped.

But then I hear the word again, distinctly this time, ringing through the enormous building like an echo in a canyon.

*Help!*

It's a word humans are programmed to hear, no matter the language or circumstance, whether coming from a five-year old at a playground during a game of tag, or from a swimmer struggling in the ocean. The word rings softly, almost inaudibly, but I can see in the eyes of Jones and Smalley that they've heard it too.

"Is that them?" I ask, looking at Pam, my voice piercing with urgency. "The internals?"

"I guess," Pam says, looking confused, a tone of irritation in her voice, as if helping these people wasn't part of their deal and thus she doesn't want to focus on them.

"Where are they, Pam?" I return to my professor voice, but underneath it the bubbles are forming, and it won't take much to bring them to the surface.

"I...I don't know. I said I would take you back to the rink. To the penalty box. I'll take you to Stella and the colonel and we can—"

"What did you say?" I hear the words come from my mouth, but I feel like they've been spoken by some alien being on another planet. I can feel the blood rush from my face, my knees weakening. I could faint if I'm not careful, so I force myself to rally from the blow of her words.

"I don't know where the internals are, but—"

"The name you just gave. Who did you say?"

"What? Oh, Ms. Wyeth. Estelle Wyeth. She goes by Stella. We don't usually call her by her first name because—"

"I don't care." I pivot to Jones. "Give me the gun, Mr. Jones."

Jones hands me the gun without hesitation. He no doubt recognizes the determination that has suddenly overcome me, perhaps from some past experience of his own when a thing needed done at the moment without question.

"This wasn't the deal." Pam complains. "I'm not sure—"

I raise the gun and point it at Sydney.

"Whoa, professor, what's going on?" It's Smalley, her tone more curious than concerned.

"Where are they? Where *exactly* are the internals?"

"I...I don't know. I mean, we can hear them, so they obviously must be close, but they weren't in one of the offices so I don't know."

I study Pam's face for a few seconds. "I think you're lying."

Pam puts her hands on her hips and cocks her head, and then opens her eyes wide, defiantly. "Well I'm not."

I open my eyes equally wide now and take a step toward Sydney. "Well, we're going to find out. I'm counting to two, and if you haven't told me where they are, I'm shooting your friend in the face."

"Jesus, Dom," Jones says. "What just happened?" I can hear the doubt in his voice, doubt that maybe him giving me the gun wasn't the best idea after all.

I ignore him, my focus locked now on the young IT specialist, Sydney, who was probably considering grad school only a year or two ago, and decided to go with this job instead. She's crouched in a heap below me, facing forward and crying to some unseen god.

"This place is too big and I don't have time to look around. And suddenly I don't trust you anymore. So here we go Pam. On two. One."

"Who counts to two?" Smalley whispers to herself rhetorically.

"It's in the floor, behind the holding cells." Pam shakes her head as she speaks, her voice distant, undetached, as if understanding that she's sealed her fate.

"What is?"

Pam rolls her eyes. "The blueprints to Fort Knox. What are we talking about? The people who came with Ms. Wyeth. They're in a cellar behind the offices."

Stella.

The name suddenly hits me again. I knew it. And then for a while I didn't know it. But I think I always did. Somewhere inside of me, I knew Stella was lying. Or at least holding something back. Maybe I didn't think it was something on this scale, but I knew there was more to her story.

*A man and his son.* Or grandson. That's who Pam said were with them. That means Tom and James.

And no Danielle, which means Danielle is dead. What other explanation could there be?

"If those two men aren't out of that cellar in the next two minutes, I'm going to tie a rope around you and young Sydney here, and the three of us are going to hoist you up over the wall of office number six and into the pit of that thing back there."

"I don't understand what the hell happened here?" Pam asks, genuinely confused. "I thought we had a deal. What did we do wrong?" She looks at Jones, who can only shrug, not quite understanding the change in terms himself.

"You took the wrong job, Pam, and then the wrong people broke into your office today. Let's go."

We walk around to the backside of the right row of offices, and as we turn the corner, I can just make out to my left, in the distance, one of the panes of glass that forms the hockey rink. I can't see any of the crabs from here, but I think I can see a section of the penalty box contraption that Pam mentioned.

At the back corner of the office row, we turn right again and circle back towards the front, and, about a third of the way back, Pam stops above a small square that's been carved into the floor. The hinges and latch are sunken so that anyone walking near it would barely notice the hatch existed. The pounding and screaming beneath has stopped.

"It's here," Pam says.

"I'm really hoping that when you open this door, my friends come out of there unharmed."

"Friends?" Smalley and Jones say simultaneously, like they've practiced the line for a slapstick comedy routine. "What are you talking about, Dom?" Jones adds.

"It's them, my group from the boat, and the diner, the ones I've been looking for. Two of them at least."

"How do you know that?"

I don't have the time or energy to explain it all now, so I close my eyes and shake off Jones' question. "Just open it, Pam."

She reaches down to the latch of the cellar and, before she places her hand on the thin metal, a voice echoes through the hangar. "Hello, Dominic."

I know instantly it's Stella, and her speech is coming from somewhere high up and behind me. The words sound powerful, nearly bringing me to my knees. But I hold myself steady and take a deep breath, resisting the urge to turn. I can't know for sure, but I'm guessing there is a rifle or two pointed at my back.

"Who the hell is that," Smalley asks, wasting no time in turning toward Stella. But she gets no reply from the woman.

Jones is already facing in that direction and I can see his eyes searching for the voice as well.

It's Sydney's turn to rotate to the voice now, and I can hear the relief in her weak and pleading voice when she says, "Ms. Wyeth." She pauses and lets out an audible bawling sniffle. "Oh my god, Ms. Wyeth! They broke in and took us—"

"I've no doubt you did all you could, Sydney," Stella interrupts, and I can hear in her tone that she's clearly embarrassed by the girl.

"Where are you?" Jones asks, and with that question, I turn in time to see Stella walk from an unlit section of the raised walkway into the halo of the auxiliary lights below; walking beside her are two soldiers, presumably the ones who monitor the roof for hordes.

"As I'm sure you did too, Ms. Young." Stella is too far away for me to see her eyes, but I can almost feel the look of contempt in them, blazing at the back of Pam like lasers. "And where is Spencer?"

Pam turns now and looks up at Stella, shaking her head. "He left. He just...they broke in through the lobby glass and then he...I don't know."

Stella nods at Pam's answer, a gesture that says she always suspected Spencer would betray her someday, though betrayal wasn't quite what it was.

Stella moves a few steps closer on the walkway, so that her face is now fully illuminated by the light. Her hair is pulled back and her face made up. She looks showered, freshly clothed.

"Where's Danielle?" I command, stepping away from the door to the underground prison and toward Stella, meeting her eyes with mine as I approach.

"That's good right there, Dominic." The soldiers don't move, but the message has been sent.

I can see Stella's face even clearer now, but there isn't the look of smugness I had expected, a look that says *you were right not to trust me, Dominic, and you should have gone with that feeling.* Her look is worse than self-satisfied. It's cold and uncaring. All business.

"Answer me, Stella. Where is she?" Suddenly, the whereabouts of Danielle is the only thing I'm interested in. The rest of it—the 'Whys' and the 'Whos' of everything that went on in this building, and even Tom and James imprisoned below me—has now taken a secondary position.

"She's pretty amazing isn't she?" Stella asks, nodding in what appears to be genuine appreciation for Danielle's aptitude. "After Tom got that boat started and got us to shore, it was mostly Danielle who kept us alive for the next few days. Though I'd be misconveying the story if I gave her all of the credit. Some of it has to go to Tom as well. Maybe even a little bit to James." She folds her hands in front of her and erects her posture. "Certainly none of the credit goes to you though, Dom. I see you've moved on and made new friends."

I feel no need to defend myself to Stella, but I would be lying if said I don't feel the tiniest of stings from her jab. If I had found a way back on the cruiser, maybe Danielle would still be alive.

Stella looks at Pam and frowns. "Are you going to open the door or what?"

"Okay," Pam answers quickly, timidly, and then she un-latches the door to the cellar, pulling it up and flopping it to the floor.

I walk over to the opening and look inside, and there, on the floor about ten feet below ground level, are Tom and James sitting against the tight, metal walls of the enclosure. Their eyes are closed and they look haggard and skinny, in dire need of a meal. I immediately note their shoes, which are not on their feet, and I quickly realize the banging was coming from them throwing the footwear up against the bottom of the cellar door. It was likely that physical strain and their cries for help that have now tired them to the point of exhaustion.

"Jesus Christ, Stella," I say, shooting a glare toward the woman that's as poisonous as the thoughts in my head. I take a single step toward her, this time with aggression, and I can see the soldier to Stella's left raise his rifle and point.

And then I hear a voice from below.

"She made it out."

I can hear immediately that it's James, his speech weary and dry, and I move back to the opening. I have no concern for the weapon pointed at me—I assume the endgame involves me dying, though probably not like this—and I can see James is slightly less slumped than before. His eyes are still closed and his breathing is labored and slow.

"She made it out, Dom. They tried to get her, but..." James coughs a couple of hoarse, painful coughs. "But she's a badass."

I doubt Stella can understand the words James is saying, not from the distance she's standing, but she can definitely hear that he is saying something, and I don't want to risk him getting shot for spilling any secrets he may have, though what harm they would do at this point I can't imagine.

"Good James," I whisper down. I look over at Pam, who's standing only two or three feet from me, and I give her a stare that threatens murder. "We'll find her, buddy. Just hang in there."

"What is he saying?" Stella calls down from her perch, and I can hear a trace of concern in the question.

"He's delirious," I call back, and I realize that I'm not sure that isn't the truth. "He's dying Stella. And being in that cold pit is only going to speed that up."

"He'll be fine."

I shake my head and chuckle softly. "Man, Stella, you are quite the thespian. I mean it. I taught English literature for eight years, at the college level, and I saw lots of Shakespeare and Ibsen and O'Neill. But I don't know that I've ever seen a performance like you pulled off."

Stella purses her lips, as if accepting my words as a compliment.

"I mean, I always knew you were a bitch, which I'm pretty sure you knew I always knew; but I thought there might be a small pocket of decency inside you somewhere."

"What the hell do you know about decency?" Stella snaps, clearly fed up with my indignation, especially considering she's the one with the guns. "How many times did you cheat on your wife, Dom? A *decent* amount of times? And then the woman you left her for, how decent was it of you to let her die out in the snow, ravaged by monsters?"

"Monsters that you created," I remind, but it lands with little effect. Still, the fact that Stella is pointing out my flaws and indiscretions as a way to justify her own brutality leads me to reconsider that perhaps at least has the remnants of a conscience; otherwise, why would she be wasting her breath?

"If we could have conducted this experiment without anyone dying—or changing—don't you think I would have chosen that route instead?"

I shrug and answer honestly. "I don't know, Stella. I have no idea what to think about you. I mean, you're obviously evil, I just don't know exactly how far into hell you go."

She rolls her eyes and shakes me off dismissively, as if my answer is a childish one.

"Experimentation is a messy thing sometimes. Especially in this industry. And this particular experiment was simply necessary. It was the only way we could know the full impact, the global impact."

The more Stella reveals to me, to us, the more I know for sure she doesn't have any intention of letting us live. "The global impact of what?"

"Our product, Dom."

"Your product?"

Stella steels her look now. "That's right. Our product. The result of decades of work by geniuses in fields ranging from chemistry to anthropology. And unfortunately, I don't have the time to explain it and you don' have the capacity to understand it even if I did. No offense on that last part; it's just that there's a lot of advanced science involved that I fear it would sound a lot like Greek to the untrained ear."

I have so many questions my head is ringing, about the chemical and the explosion and the snow and the reasons for the changes. But Stella's demeanor gives me the feeling that my time to ask questions is nearing the end, so I cut to the ones most important to me. "How are you doing this? How could you destroy so much and be able to explain it to the rest of the world?"

Stella shrugs. "It's not easy. Every day is a mammoth effort by our PR people to satisfy the press. But we have extremely charismatic and persuasive people in our company, people who earn a lot of money to explain things satisfactorily. But it's also perhaps not as difficult as you might think. There are more than enough bad people in even worse countries all over the world. And plenty of their surrogates here at home. It's hard to satisfy the details the families and the press and the politicians demand, but it isn't hard to find someone to take the rap."

I shake my head, hearing the words but still not quite believing it all. "But you've got a whole county cordoned off. More than one county. Even if you can convince people that thousands are dead or missing, how can you keep that going?"

"She has an army son."

It's the colonel from the exit ramp. I notice his stature and facial structure the moment he steps from the shadows and past Stella. But he doesn't remain on the scaffolding; instead, he climbs down the ladder, moving with the grace of a gymnast, despite being in what must be his late-fifties. He hops to the ground, turning towards me on the dismount.

"It's a fact that history has proven over and over again: people trust the military force on the ground. Even the generals and politicians in charge of that force don't question it, at least not in the beginning. After all, what choice is there? A bomb went off in Warren County, and those of us on the scene, the elite squadron of soldiers who happened to be conducting exercises there at the time, well we've decided the area is no longer safe to occupy. We're working on getting all of the names of the people affected, of course, but until then, we can't risk allowing anyone inside. Think Chernobyl, something of that magnitude. That's what the world envisions now when they hear Warren County. There's a whole lot of radiation and instability inside, and that's all people need to hear to keep as far away from this place as possible. We tried to pick a time when the fewest people would be affected, but there's really no way to do that with an area this large."

"So you're the heroes then?" I take a step forward, feeling a primal need to exert some measure of counter-masculinity. "Blame some fanatic from ten thousand miles away, and then sacrifice yourselves for the cleanup."

The colonel smiles a huge toothy smile that stretches temple-to-temple. "You're damn right, son. Who else would be willing to clean up this cancer-infested cluster-fuck?"

It's a rhetorical question, but I shake my head, indicating that no one would.

"And fortunately, as Ms. Wyeth alluded to, we didn't need to search ten thousand miles. We were able to find a fanatic right here in town. Eastern European—Muslim, but with blonde hair and blue eyes. That way everyone is happy. He'll be as infamous as Hitler when this is over."

"Who are you? Where do you get this authority?"

"It's a long, thin chain of command, son. That's about all I can say about it."

I look back to Stella. "So how does this end? What's the point?"

Stella nods, satisfied with the inquiry. "That question, the 'why' part of all of this, is the last question we ask at D&W. Our sponsor never gives us a reason, and we don't ask for one."

The colonel picks up from Stella and continues the answer, as if completing the second half of a motto. "Create something new and powerful, and we'll figure out how to use it. Those are the specs."

I feel nauseous and I want to sit, but instead I lean over slowly and put my hands on my knees. I keep my head up, facing forward, trying to breathe.

The colonel takes a few more steps in our direction now, walking casually, his tight lapels and rows of medals making him look like an actor in some Vietnam drama. He steps past me and takes a quick peek into the pit, giving a mildly curious 'Hmm,' as if he's seeing Tom and James for the first time in their new accommodations. He then saunters over and stops directly in front of Smalley. "Hello, specialist Smalley."

Smalley's eyes get wide as she takes a swallow, and then she looks over to Jones first, then to me, and then finally to the ground.

"Did you think I wouldn't recognize you?" the colonel asks, a bemused smile on his face.

Smalley stays quiet.

"I never forget my soldiers, even the ones who were under my command for as short a time as you were."

Smalley stays quiet.

"And I always give my soldiers a second chance, that's another thing my men and women know about me." The colonel pauses and dips his chin, and a rigid, compelling stare forms beneath his brow. "We could use more bodies here, Smalley, especially those who've been out there, who've been in the fight."

"What the hell is going on, Smalley?" Jones asks. "You know this piece of shit? You were under his command? When?"

For a moment, I think the colonel is going to rush Jones and snap his neck with his bare hands. I can't imagine someone as intense as the man standing before me letting a remark like that slide. But he doesn't react a bit.

"This was my story, Jones," Smalley says. "I just never told you the details. Special orders. Top secret. Orders were for peacekeeping, but I knew that was a lie. I found out what was happening three days into my tour, and then, during one of our missions into the interior, I walked away. They didn't abandon me, I went AWOL."

Smalley pauses and blinks a few times, clearing her thoughts.

"I thought since I knew the perimeter and where the snipers were that I'd be able to get us out that day. But they reinforced everything. It was my fault, Jones, it was my fault we lost all those people that day. And you don't ever talk about it, but it was my fault. I was the one who suggested we go that direction."

"It wasn't your fault, Smalley. I never blamed you for a second. But...why didn't you tell me about this?"

"I don't know. It was stupid. The rest of you had similar stories about being left in the cordon, abandoned, so I adjusted my story. I thought otherwise you might think I was some kind of spy or something. And then it just got too far in to change. I'm sorry, Jones."

"We never discussed this," Stella says to the colonel, breaking up the internal revelation between Jones and Smalley. "And we have way too many loose ends as it is."

I can't know for sure, but something tells me the loose ends she's referring to are Pam and Sydney.

"Ah, but see that's where you're wrong," the colonel says, smiling, never taking his eyes off Stephanie, who looks as humbled and uncomfortable as a prisoner of war. "Specialist Smalley is no loose end."

Smalley looks over at me now, tears in her eyes. "I'm sorry."

"Don't apologize, soldier!" the colonel shouts. He's in Smalley's face now, spittle flying.

Jones steps over to wedge himself between the two soldiers, and without a second's pause, the colonel thrusts his knee into Jones' groin, sending him to his knees with a thud. Jones keeps his back straight, despite the trauma, and I can see the butt of the pistol sticking from the small of his back.

I'd forgotten about the gun, and to this point, no one from Stella's team has thought to check us for weapons. I'm still adorned with the backpack containing the various supplies from the grocery store, including the knives and flares.

"Don't step to me, son. I don't know what unit you're from, but I'd suggest you never step to a ranking officer that way."

"Fuck you," Jones manages, though it's barely audible through his pain.

Smalley meets her colonel's eyes now, and I can see the tension that's built up in her jaws. "Yeah, Colonel Marsh, fuck you."

The colonel stares coldly at Smalley and, for a moment, I think she's about to meet a similar fate as Jones, perhaps with a backhanded slap to the face instead. But the colonel just smiles and turns back to Stella. "I guess you're right, Ms. Wyeth, it looks like we can continue with the experiments as planned."

"What are you going to do?" I ask.

"What do you think, Hemingway?" the colonel asks. "Take a few guesses. I bet you'll never get it?"

I ignore him and stay locked on Stella. "I assume you plan on killing us, but what else? Are you going to turn us into these things?"

"Look at that!" the colonel shouts, as if I've landed on a jackpot at a casino.

"I know you've noticed the snow, Dominic, how it's melting. Slowly, but it is melting. And there's no more coming, at least not of the variety we created. And our new creations don't do well in the warm air. You may have seen our resident example on your way through the corridor."

The gray creature in the office. I nod.

"They need the snow for life. The chemical that laced the initial snowfall caused their change, but it's the snow itself that keeps them alive. They need it, like a great white needs the salt of the ocean. But it also makes them lethargic and docile. That is until, as you know all too well, they get agitated or intrigued enough to attack." Stella looks up and to the side, pondering. "We haven't quite nailed down what qualifies as intriguing to them, not yet, but we think we're getting closer. However, we have a dilemma. A paradox I suppose."

"And what is that?"

"Now that the snow is melting, they're becoming more aggressive. They feel threatened, we think. Perhaps it's pain, we're not sure, and they're lashing out in ways they haven't to this point. They don't need the sound of crashing glass or the approach of a person anymore, they're just attacking."

"So what does any of this mean exactly? We're all screwed, I take it?"

"Soon the snow will melt and they'll eventually die. But in the meantime, in that transition phase, they're expressing the aggression that we've been trying to harness, the combative qualities that will be useful to our sponsor." Stella motions to the colonel. "Therefore, in our new batch, we're hoping to find that proper balance that will keep them alive but also aggressive, even after the snows have gone."

"New batch? What the hell are you talking about? You just said they're dying? That's what you need to let happen. Even if you kill us, Stella, you can't do this again. How many people can you kill? And do you really think you can keep exploding bombs in small towns and explain it all away with terrorism?"

Stella shakes her head matter-of-factly. "No. No, of course not. We've purchased other islands around the world—on behalf of our sponsor, naturally—and that's where we plan to perfect things. Obviously the citizens of this country can buy this story only once. Twice would be a bridge too far, I think."

Stella stops again and looks to some distant spot, considering that this could happen again. Another terror attack, perhaps.

"But in the meantime," she continues, "during the melting, we can still do a lot of work here in the lab. There's so much more to learn about their behavior, why they attack, how they change. And that's where you come in. Though, honestly, you and your friends are a bonus, Dom. I was thinking we would just have Tom and James to work with—and Pam and Stella, of course."

Pam's eyes immediately shoot wide and she begins to shake her head. "No. You said you needed us for—"

"For what, Pam? IT. This entire place is run remotely from Headquarters. You're here for just the purpose I've intimated. You always have been."

"My family knows I wasn't in the blast. They know I've been flying in, working on the 'cleanup.'" Pam makes the air quotes, again with the last two fingers on each hand.

"And your family will be sad to learn of your disappearance somewhere in the interior. You were following Spence, of course. You two *were* sleeping together, right?"

"No," Sydney cries. "You can't do this." And as she says her last word, she turns and races toward the door that opens into the long corridor that leads out to the lobby, never looking back.

I see the soldiers raise their guns, followed by Stella shouting, "No!"

The two soldiers lower their weapons and shoulder them, and then race down the ladder and in the direction of Sydney. The first one takes a wide path through the office corridor, but the other takes the more direct path, coming right toward me and the open cellar.

And that's when I make my move.

As the soldier reaches the start of the cellar, just as he begins to pass me, I thrust out my hip and shoulder, and catch him squarely on the right side of his body. The collision almost sends him airborne, and he careens toward the hole, flailing.

His left foot goes in first, and he nearly drops to the bottom of the pit like a bag of sand; but as his body begins to slide down, sending him in completely, he manages to grab the ledge of the cellar with his right hand. For a moment his right foot catches the ledge as well, which would have kept him in a position to climb up, but it slowly drops in by his left, and now he's hanging on with only his hands, his dead weight below him.

And the gun has dropped straight down to the floor past him.

I turn to see the colonel grab for his pistol, but it's too late for him—Jones has his own pistol aimed at the man's chest. "You blink and you're dead, motherfucker. And I'm really hoping you blink."

I walk to the opening of the cellar and look down at Tom and James, who are both beginning to stir, awakened by the ruckus above and the rifle that's fallen in a clatter beside them. "Tom!" I call.

"Help me, you bastard," the soldier says to me, his voice pleading and desperate despite the impoliteness of his words.

I reach down as if to grab his hand, hoping he'll hang on long enough for one of the two men below to grab the gun. The fall will be a painful one for the soldier, but not likely fatal, and if he's able to secure the gun, he'll have Tom and James hostage and me in a tricky position.

The dangling soldier falls for the ploy, perhaps underestimating my own will to survive and to sacrifice him in the process, and as he slides his hand ever so slightly toward me, raising the tips of his fingers, searching for my grasp like an ant's antennae, I call again, "Tom!," this time loud and authoritative.

The old man's eyes open with a start. There's life in them, awareness.

"Grab that gun, Tom."

He nods, shaking away the cobwebs from his brain, and he picks up the weapon and instinctively locks the next round into place. "Let him fall."

"No!" the soldier cries, and before the word has completely left the back of his throat, I nudge the toe of my boot to the fingers of his left hand, and he plummets to the ground below with a splat.

# Chapter 12

One soldier is down and the colonel is contained. That leaves the second soldier who is currently in pursuit of Sydney. And Smalley is only a step behind him. There's not a lot I can do to improve that situation other than to put my faith in Smalley.

Which leaves only Stella.

I have no idea if Stella is armed, but based on the flanking soldiers that were standing beside her less than two minutes ago, I'm guessing she's not. She's the scientist after all, and I get the impression that she would consider guns beneath her.

In all of the mayhem, however, she's managed to disappear.

I check back on the men down in the cellar, and I can tell that the soldier is in bad shape, at least on his right leg from the knee down. His tibia is clearly broken, the white of the bone is glimmering and flecked with blood. He's writhing in pain, and the sound coming from him is that of a wounded vixen, perhaps one caught in a hunter's trap. But Tom is unmoved by the howls of agony and holds the gun steady and aimed, looking twitchy, ready to shoot.

"Hold on, Tom, I'm gonna get you guys out. How did they get you down there in the first place?"

"Had a rope ladder of some kind. Just flopped it over the side and forced us down."

I look at Pam, but she shrugs and shakes her head, indicating she doesn't know the whereabouts of the ladder.

I turn to the colonel, who stands as if bored by the whole display that's unfolding, mildly frustrated that he's allowed someone to get the drop on him. "Where's the ladder?" I demand.

The colonel squints and gives a thoughtful pose, looking up to the ceiling in contemplation, and then says, "You know, the last time I saw it I think it was up your ass."

I feel a primeval urge to move on the colonel, but before I can take a step, Jones is in front of him, the barrel of the pistol against the middle of the colonel's forehead.

The colonel closes his eyes, his mouth a flat, sterile line of resolve. "Do it."

Instead of firing, Jones slams his knee up into the colonel's groin and then pushes him away. The colonel reels back a few steps and then collapses to the floor, rolling to his side in the fetal position.

The assault is pure satisfaction, but it doesn't help me with the ladder, though judging by the way the colonel looked down at Tom and James on his way over to Smalley, I'm fairly sure he doesn't know where it is anyway.

"I'm going to secure this asshole and then go track down Smalley," Jones says. "There's plenty of material here to keep him tied up for a while." Stewart Jones gives me the look of a general, though I never did get the background on his rank or who he is exactly. "Pam, I need you to track down that ladder and get it down to them."

"How will we get him out?" she asks, obviously referring to the soldier.

"Not at the top of my list of concerns, Pam. We'll do our best. First things first, though." Jones ducks his head a bit so that he is at perfect eye level with the woman. "Find the ladder."

Pam gives a wide-eyed nod, indicating she'll at least give it her best shot.

Jones looks at me. "Go find her, professor."

"You find her too, Jones. Find Smalley. We're getting out of this place."

Jones and I give simultaneous nods, and as we begin on our separate missions, a banging sound rings from the back of the hangar, near the rink. No doubt it's Stella, and I hold the possibility high that she's trying to lure me.

"Be careful, Dominic," Jones says, and then, apropos of nothing, looks down and gives a quick shake of his head followed by a smirk. "I wonder what it would have been like to grow up with a name like 'Dominic.' Pretty cool, I would imagine."

"Well, Stewart, I suppose it made me softer than if I had ended up with something less cool. Maybe instead of being a teacher—with all the air conditioning and summers off—I would have been a hard-ass soldier like you."

Jones gives me a piercing stare now. "You're far from soft, professor. Now let's do this." And with that, he takes off down the corridor toward the front of the building, following in the wake of Sydney and Smalley and the second soldier.

I move quickly but cautiously toward the sound in the back, and when I reach the hockey rink and look through the glass, I'm immediately mesmerized by the white crabs milling around inside. The snow lining the rink is high, up to their shins in some areas, and when they move, they're as slow as sloths.

"I'm here, Stella," I call to the emptiness beside the rink, "so tell me how you want to play this? Before you answer though, full disclosure, you should know that your colonel buddy is in zip ties, and one of your soldiers has a shattered leg and is staring at the business end of his own rifle. And in another minute, I'll have the other one too."

I wait for a reply, but none comes.

"This is over," I continue. "The experiments, the company, all of it. You'll go down as the biggest mass murderer in the history of the country. But lucky for you, it's this country, and you might get to live."

A few of the crabs look over at me through the glass, apparently responding to the sound of my voice, wearing the same expressionless look they always seem to have. At least until they're activated, triggered to aggression.

But these crabs seem virtually harmless in this frozen environment. The temperature is frigid back here, even on this side of the glass, and it's clearly the snow and cold that has these crabs so calm, just like Stella said.

It's the warming that agitates them and turns them nasty.

And with the warming comes the melting.

It's already started, Stella revealed as much. The snow is disappearing, and when it's all gone, the crabs will die. But in the meantime, as they go through their transition from docility to death, they become the ravenous monsters from the student union, the ones that formed a ladder of their bodies and came in through the shattered window on the day Naia and I left.

The thought of the crabs' almost certain demise buoys me though. The world hasn't come to an end after all. We, in Warren and Maripo County were simply the unfortunate chosen ones on whom an almost indescribable madness was tested. But it's ending, soon, and now we need only to wait out the virtual spring that is right around the corner. They'll be no more explosions, no more chemicals released into the air which turn the sky to white and then release fluffy flakes of poison.

I walk further around the perimeter of the egg-shaped rink until I come to a door in the middle of one of the long sections. The door opens into a tunnel that leads out into a round room in the middle of the rink. From that central room, I can see that several other walkways radiate out in four or five different directions, like the spokes of a wheel, which end in similar rooms to the hub in the middle. This is the penalty box, I presume.

The walkways and rooms are open at the top, but there is a protective glass, which starts about three-feet high and extends up at least ten feet.

The rink door that opens into the main walkway is closed, but, judging by the unlocked deadbolt and the accompanying chain that snakes limply from the door to the floor, it's accessible.

I walk past the door toward the back of the rink, where, about fifteen feet past, a giant wall rises from the floor to the massively high ceiling, and extends across the entire width of the hangar, cutting off this section of the hangar from the rest. It looks almost identical to the wall that separated the lobby from the section of the hangar I'm in currently, though this one seems to be made of concrete.

I walk up to the wall and place my hands against it, feeling the cold, black stone against my palms. The side of the wall I'm on is only a fraction of the entire building, so whatever is on the other side makes up probably three-quarters of the rest of the facility. I can see a door in the wall about twenty paces to my left, and I'd like nothing more than to enter to the other side.

But I can't spend time exploring now. Right now, I need to find Stella.

I turn around now, and, as if the thought of my former companion was itself a summons, I see Stella standing against the rink. The second soldier, the one who was chasing Sydney, is standing beside her, his rifle high on his soldier and pointed at my chest.

Sydney is below him on the floor, her feet and hands tied. Smalley and Jones are nowhere to be seen.

"Curiosity killed the cat, Dominic. You don't really want to go over there anyway. That's where the helicopter lands, and you never quite know when it's coming. They tell us one day, but it's usually the wrong one. I think they keep us guessing on purpose." Stella looks over at the soldier. "Escort him to the penalty box, Aaron," she says.

"Where are they?" I demand. "What happened to Jones and Smalley?"

Stella shrugs and then nods to the soldier, giving him permission to answer.

The soldier mimics Stella's shrug and says, "Sydney was easy to catch, she's back in—"

"I don't give a damn about Sydney!" I interrupt, yelling now. "Where the hell are my friends?"

The soldier pauses and says calmly, "They ran right past me. I caught Stella, stood behind the door, and watched them chase after me into the lobby. I thought about picking them off from behind, couple of shots to the head, but that could have gotten messy, maybe even led to some kind of firefight. It was easier just to lock them out. They're on the outside again. Without the code, there's nothing they can do to get back in."

They're not dead, that's the takeaway. I may never see Jones and Smalley again, but at least they have a chance to get out once the melting takes place and this ultimately ends. I have to believe that.

"Let's go," the soldier named Aaron commands, and he motions me back toward the entrance to the penalty box. He stops me in front of the door, and Stella continues walking on, back toward the corridor between the offices.

I watch her go, and then look at Aaron. "Do you know what's happened, Aaron? On the outside, I mean? I guess you do, right? How could you not?"

Aaron keeps his eyes fixed and demeanor stoical.

"You're going to die, soldier, and I don't mean fifty years from now. This event, and your complicity in it, is going to be what kills you. But you can do the right thing before you go. And maybe by doing the right thing you'll save yourself, who knows?"

The soldier blinks and shifts his jaw to the left, a sign that maybe my words are at least having a small effect on the man's conscience. He says nothing.

I turn back to the hockey rink and study again the desultory beasts inside. Nineteen of them, that's what Pam said, and there seems to be no pattern or reason to their clusters or movements. They look despondent, hopeless, and for the first time in ages, I recall that all of these things were people once, people who had friends and families, many of whom were spared from this cataclysm and now live somewhere on the outside mourning the death of their loved ones.

But they're not dead. Not quite. They still have working muscles and organs, lungs to breathe and hearts to pump blood. And they feel pain, perhaps the most indicative quality of animal life.

But though they aren't dead, these crabs, these beings that I've come to fear and hate and pity, are not human. Not anymore. They're modern-day mutants, humans that have devolved into mindless, speechless savages. With many of the same characteristics, yes, but different in too many ways to continue calling them human.

Lost in the existential thoughts of these beings, I'm brought back to the present moment by the sound of a grunt from behind me, followed by the sound of Stella's voice, barking commands.

I turn back and look across the hangar to the corridor of offices, and there, emerging from the long hallway, is the aggressive gray crab from office six. The crab is hunched over, not on all fours the way they tend to move naturally, but bent at the waist, like some beat-down geek from a turn-of-the-century circus. Stella is behind the crab, barking at the creature as she pushes her arms forward, shoving them towards the back of the crab's head.

As Stella and the twisted crab approach me, it starts to come into focus what is happening. There's a shackle around the crab's neck, a manacle, and coming from the back of the metal bond is a long, stiff bar that stretches at least five feet before ending in Stella's hands.

Stella and the beast move quickly toward me, almost running now, and for a moment, I think Stella is going to pull back on some trigger and release the crab from its metal bind, allowing its momentum to send it towards me in all its rage. And with the armed soldier still present, serving as Stella's protection, this possibility seems very real.

Instead, they just continue coming, Stella shoving and agitating the crab with every thrust, the thing's black eyes, normally expressionless, wrinkled in anger as it tries to turn its neck back to the source of the agitation. But the device in Stella's hand makes it impossible for the crab to turn, frustrating it further.

Stella suddenly stops the crab about eight feet from me. The thing is about at the level of my waist, and it doesn't meet my eyes, so preoccupied is it on the metal constraint around its neck.

"Open it," Stella says to me, motioning to the penalty box. She pushes down on the rod and lowers the crab's head almost to the ground, holding the tool in position the way one would hold a shovel in preparation for digging a hole.

"What are you going to do, Stella?" I ask, having some idea.

"I told you I wasn't done. There's so much more to learn from them, more to study. Now open the door and get inside. I won't be stalled. I know time is running out for me, but it can still happen."

I'm not quite sure what 'it' means in Stella's sentence, but I take a deep breath and turn to the door of the rink, opening it and stepping through to the walkway that leads down into the hub in the middle. I shut the door behind me.

"I didn't tell you to close the door, Dominic."

I don't respond or move to re-open the door.

"Move to the center and stay there."

I hold Stella's eyes a moment longer, thinking of something to say, something that will persuade her to re-think the murder she's about to commit. But I can see there's only madness behind them.

"Shoot him, Aaron." Stella says calmly.

I raise my hands immediately in surrender, staving off Aaron's shot. I can see the look of doubt in the soldier's eyes, and the relief at not having to squeeze the trigger. I walk slowly to the hub, but I when I reach the middle of it, I turn around quickly, watching the entrance with angst, nearly hyperventilating as I wait to see the unfolding of my execution.

Aaron lowers the rifle and opens the door to the penalty box, and then takes a huge step to the side as Stella shoves the metal rod forward, pushing the crab's head and neck until it reluctantly creeps inside the contained area. Then, with a yank of her rear hand, she releases the claws of the manacle from the crab's neck.

The crab instantly spins back toward Stella and lunges at her, but Aaron is quick with the door, closing it just in time and bouncing the beast back inside the walkway.

The creature attacks the door relentlessly for a full thirty seconds, at least, but then, getting no results, it finally turns to the open space that stretches out in front of it. I stand at the end of that space with my heart racing like a hummingbird's, and a brief flash of my mortality enters my mind, a recognition that my life is going to end in a matter of seconds. And there's little doubt to it, really. I don't have the strength to fight this thing, and I'm not sure there's a human alive who would. It would be like grappling with a deranged chimpanzee; maybe the strongest man in the world could deal with it, but that's not me.

And there's no real chance of escape. I'm literally trapped. No matter which one of the five tunnels I run down, once I get to the end of it, there's nowhere to go from there.

My mind suddenly clears, and I think of my backpack, which, miraculously, is still in my possession. I don't remember exactly what's inside still, so before I make my final flight for life and sprint down one of the spoked sections, I fling my bag from my back and unzip the main part of the case.

And with the sound of the zipper, the crab drops to all fours and starts running.

I sprint to the spoke that extends in a ten o'clock direction from the hub, rifling through the bag as I go. I reach the end of the spoke quickly, and immediately the crabs that are on the ice begin to move toward me in curiosity. I don't know if it's because I'm new to the chamber, or because of my frantic motion, but their energy has definitely lifted, and I can see now how the design of these chambers are perfect for observing the creatures, much the same way those walkthrough hamster-style tubes are popular in some high-end aquariums.

I stand with my back pressed against the far wall of the spoke, looking back toward the penalty box entrance and down the main walkway, trying to gauge where the crab has run. But my view is now obscured by the angle of the spoke, and with the crab down on all fours, I can't see over the walls of the walkways. The beast could be anywhere now.

And then I hear Stella yell, "That's good, Dom, keep running. And feel free to hide, though I know there isn't much to shield you. But that's what I want to see: how long it takes for him to find you. Oh, and when he does, please fight. It will add to the research."

I'm hoping the cold air of the hockey rink will slow the creature down, even if only slightly, just to give me a chance to escape when it eventually does come in my direction.

*Feel free to hide.* It's not a bad idea. I don't have anything to block me, but I don't need to be standing high above the walls of the box, exposing myself to everyone. Thanks for the suggestion, Stella.

I crouch down below the level of the windows, hoping to give myself another few seconds to figure something out before the creature comes barreling down my spoke. I continue to rifle through my backpack, trying to keep as quiet as I can, and then, as if my hand has come upon Merlin's magic wand, I feel the papery outer lining of a flare.

I pull the flare out and hold it in front of me, unlit, and then begin to creep back toward the entrance, hoping to catch the crab off guard, poised to light the flare and stab it if the opportunity presents itself.

From my stooped position, I now can't see anything happening outside of this particular spoke, but I creep back toward the central hub of the penalty box anyway. I can't see Stella or the crab, but that means I'm invisible to them as well.

I close my eyes and take three more steps. I'm now back in the hub.

# Chapter 13

As I turn the corner into the hub, I hold the flare in front of me, ready to twist the cap and bring the spark of death to life. But I see the backside of the crab as it heads off in the direction of a different hub, chimp-walking down the spoke that radiates in the opposite direction from the one I'm exiting.

I stand up straight again, wasting no time as I jog into the corridor that leads back to the penalty box entrance, where Stella and Aaron are standing outside of the closed door. The soldier has his gun at his hip, which means the door is locked.

"Obviously it wasn't going to be that easy, Dominic," Stella calls through the glass.

The sound of Stella's voice prompts me to check my back, my assumption being that her voice would resonate through the chambers of the penalty box like an opera house auditorium.

And I'm right. From the end of the spoke that radiates to the two o'clock position, I see the crab suddenly pop into sight, standing upright, searching.

Its eyes meet mine from the back compartment of the hub, and, with little more than the time it takes to blink, the crab drops to all fours and begins heading back towards me.

I run up toward the entrance until I'm almost in arms reach of the door and yell, "Let me out, Stella!"

"Sorry, Dominic," she says, a thin smile across her face. "Give it your best shot."

I wait for the crab to enter the main corridor and then I twist the cap of the flare, sparking the dull red baton to life.

There's a trace of fear in the crab's eyes, but it's nothing like the reaction I get from the crabs in the rink on the other side of the box. Their howling starts immediately, and they all begin to cluster together, hugging the furthest side of the rink, trying to get as far from the fire as possible, despite it being no danger to them from where I stand currently.

The crab standing before me, however, shows only a fraction of his brethren's fear, and I can only imagine this reduced panic is the result of some long, brutal form of conditioning. It edges closer to me, now all but ignoring the fire.

"Yes!" Stella whispers. "Look at it! Come on. Come on."

I jab the flare out, but the crab keeps coming, its eyes focused, full of terror and hunger.

It takes two or three quick steps towards me now and then stops, pulling back slightly, like a sprinter false starting before a race. I know at once this a test, a gauge of my reaction for when it finally decides to attack.

I push my back flat against the door now, feeling the cruel, impenetrable Lucite barrier behind me. The crab takes one more slow step forward and then lunges.

I fall to my knees and close my eyes, holding the flare up in front of me like an offering to a god. The god of death. The ghostly abomination of man.

I say a silent prayer for Naia, and then I hear the gunshot.

# Chapter 14

I don't feel the pain of the attack, and the sounds that follow the gunshot aren't the gluttonous echoes of a feeding monster, but rather the scurrying feet of a scared animal. I open my eyes to see the crab running away from me, bounding off like a dog before turning the corner at the hub, escaping back toward the far spoke of the penalty box from whence it came.

I'm not sure what's happened exactly, but instinctively I get to my feet, watching as the crab finally disappears from my sight. I pivot toward the glass of the door and see Stella with her hands raised. Face down on the floor beside her is the dead body of her soldier Aaron, a hole the size of a bullet at the back of his head.

Behind them, Tom stands with the rifle of the soldier that fell into the pit atop his shoulder, staring through the sight at Stella. James and Pam are beside him. Pam's face is locked in shock at the killing of Aaron that just took place, but she doesn't waste a tear on him. Or perhaps she has none left. "I found the ladder," is all she says.

I nod. "I see that. Thank you." And then to Tom and James, "Are you two okay?"

James nods, but Tom just steps forward, the gun poised still and straight as he approaches Stella. He stands only inches away from her and says, "Get inside, Stella."

Stella swallows as her eyes grow wide. "Tom, no."

"James," he says, motioning to him to go open the door.

James unlocks the deadbolt with the key that was resting in the lock and then swings the door open. I look back to the empty corridor once more and then step out.

"Your turn, Stella," Tom says.

"Tom, wait," I protest. "Listen, we'll take her in."

Tom shakes me off. "Gonna have to let me do this, Dom. I'm sorry; it's the way it is."

"We don't have time for this, Tom. I have to find Smalley and Jones."

Tom gives me a quizzical glance and then focuses back on Stella. "Who are they?"

"They helped me. After I left the boat. I...just trust me, Tom, I need to find them."

"Well, we'll find 'em then. But first this business. Get in, Stella."

"Shoot me," Stella says, her eyes fixed on her captor, daring Tom to squeeze off a round. "If I'm to die, I'm not dying like that."

Tom pauses, as if considering the option, and then says, "Let's go."

Stella begins to scream as James grabs her and carries her toward the penalty box entrance, and for a moment I consider a full on physical confrontation to stop it from happening.

But it never comes to that. Simultaneous with Stella's scream, almost harmonically, really, a sound like a medieval drawbridge opening roars through the hangar. It screeches loud and low, the sounds of gears and age, amplifying Stella's bellows even further. And then the second act of the ruckus follows when a whipping sound enters the symphony, drowning out the drawbridge sound like the flapping wings of some giant bird.

We all stare up in awe to the junction in the ceiling, as it's clear that the massive noise is coming from outside the hangar, above us and on the other side of the wall that divides the sections of the building.

"What the hell is that?" James yells.

"It's the roof," I call back. "The roof of the hangar is opening. And it sounds like a helicopter is landing inside."

"That's impossible," Stella says, now standing awkwardly by the door next to Tom and James, still on the verge of being sent to her death by the two men.

I look at Tom for a moment with pity. His rage has now made him a cold-blooded killer. It's likely that's what's kept him alive, but I'm saddened by his new demeanor.

"The roof can only be opened by the guard stationed on the perimeter of the roof," Stella continues. "But Aaron is dead and you said Curtis is in the cellar."

"He's dead too," Tom says, and I don't want to know the details of how that played out.

"Smalley and Jones," I say under my breath.

I can't know it's them for sure, but who else could it be? They knew that the hangar was currently unguarded, and once they were locked out and not able to get back in the building through the interior door, they must have found a way up to the roof. Maybe they even heard the approaching whir of the helicopter and it gave them the idea. There must be some exterior ladder along the side of the building for just that purpose. And with their military background and technical training, they would have figured out how to open the roof easily. It probably was no more complicated than pressing a button labeled 'OPEN.'

"They couldn't have..." Stella begins, but then cuts herself off, seemingly coming to the same conclusions I just did.

The five of us—Stella, Tom, James, Pam, and I—stand staring at the ceiling in wonder, waiting to see what happens next, waiting to see who comes through the door that leads from the landing section of the hangar. Sydney remains on the floor, looking catatonic with fear.

And then, because of the distraction of the mechanical roof and the sound of the landing helicopter, no one notices when the crab from the penalty box comes barreling down the walkway and out into the main area of the hangar.

The crab smashes into James first, grabbing him by the neck and pulling him to the ground. He scuffles with it for a moment, and then pushes the beast aside. "Shoot it!" he yells.

Tom doesn't hesitate. He swivels the rifle toward the crab, just to the left to make sure he doesn't hit James, and pops off three rounds.

The crab doesn't look like it's been hit—there's no blood or sounds of agony—and it bounds away down the corridor of offices where it was caged only minutes ago.

"It's inside," Stella whines. "It can't be loose inside." The growing sound of the helicopter landing next door nearly drowns her out, but I can hear the fear in her voice, the hysteria. She backs away into the penalty box and shuts the door in front of her, staring out the window for just a moment before turning and running for safety at the far spoke of the wheel where I was hiding earlier. Once there, she presses her back against the glass and watches us in distress.

And she makes no notice of the crabs behind her.

The flare and gunshots and screaming, along with, I suppose, the noise of the helicopter, have worked the crabs in the rink into a lather, and they begin to cluster behind the glass where Stella is standing. They're silent creatures anyway, but even if they had the roars of lions, she wouldn't have heard them over the sound of the descending helicopter. And in her petrified state, fixed as she is on the free-ranging creature somewhere in the hangar, Stella also doesn't notice when they begin to form a ladder and start scaling the wall.

"Look at that," Pam says, her tone the curiosity of someone who's witnessed a lot of behavior from these creatures and is now seeing something new and intriguing.

But it's not new to me. I've seen this scaling technique a few times now. It's an attack.

I scream for Stella to move, but she can't hear me. Not even close. And when I make a move to open the door to the box, Tom holds me back, his arms strong and secure like a father's as he brings me into his chest. And it isn't hate for Stella that's precipitated this reaction, it's a desire to protect me.

One of the crabs is already at the top of the wall and about to scale over. Even if she noticed them now, it would be too late.

The first crab grabs Stella by the face, digging its fingers into her eye sockets as it pulls up. The next one over the wall drops to the ground of the box and grips Stella at her waist, thrusting its mouth into her belly. I can see the scream, but I can't hear it, and I turn away before she's torn apart completely.

"Let's go, Dom," Tom says. "That door there, let's see if we can get through it."

But before we get halfway to the interior door, it opens from the other side, and through it walk two pilots, their hands on their heads, frowning. Behind them are Smalley and Jones.

"You guys ready to go?" Smalley asks.

I grab Sydney by the back of the shirt and lift her up, and she instinctively begins to run with the rest of the pack as we all head toward this new, open door to freedom. I look back one last time for posterity, just to imprint the lasting image of the nightmare that occurred in the D&W building. I've no doubt my testimony will be required someday, perhaps in the halls of Congress.

I take one more mental photograph, and as I turn back to the door that leads to the copter pad, I catch a glimpse of someone running.

It's the colonel.

"Wait!" he screams, the despair in his voice palpable.

I blink a few times, not quite sure I'm seeing the vision correctly.

"Wait," he repeats. "God no, wait!"

This isn't the cool, unburdened colonel from earlier, who was only mildly irritated by his captivity. But perhaps he realizes he'll be stranded here in this desolate world, and that has him spooked.

So I decide I will wait. We'll fly the colonel back to the world as a prisoner to be judged and court-martialed, and if the crimes he's committed are high enough, I'll be sure to be a witness to his execution.

But that's already been settled.

Before the colonel can make another plea, the mutant crab gallops out from the corridors and leaps onto his back, plunging its teeth into the top of the colonel's neck. He wasn't afraid of being left, he was afraid of the creature that was chasing him.

I watch for only a moment, registering yet another death into the registry of my memory, and then I follow the rest of my party through the door and out to the helicopter.

# Chapter 15

Within moments, we're back in the air, and as we lift above the hangar, I can see that the RV is no longer parked in front of the entrance to the D&W building.

Spence. He must have dodged the crabs and made it to the vehicle, and it was his lucky day when he found the keys inside.

As we fly over the cordoned-off area of Warren County, it's clear that there's more ground than snow now.

The melting is in full swing.

Many of the crabs, creatures that were once secretive and apprehensive, now run about the landscape as if rabid, fighting amongst each other, tearing at inanimate parts of the world in search of relief of the pain that the melting has brought.

And their relief will come.

In addition to the crabs roaming mad, there are the scattered corpses of others. The ones who fought their demise and lost. They're nothing more than charred outlines on the ground, and I remember the sight of Abramowitz in the receiving room of Gray's Grocery.

I don't know the whereabouts of Danielle.

She was alive when Tom and James last saw her, having escaped from Stella and the colonel only minutes into their capture. That doesn't surprise me, and my only hope now is that she survives until the melting is complete.

But survival won't be easy. The environment outside is a painting of insanity.

But Danielle is a survivor, and I hold on to hope that I'll see her again.

We fly a few miles farther, over the tanks and barriers that surround the blasted areas of the two counties, until we finally leave Maripo County for good. And as I look out the side of the helicopter and down into a foreign world of green normalcy, I begin to cry.

Dear Reader,

I hope you enjoyed The Melting.

If you're a fan of horror-inspired fairy tales, check out my Gretel Series. In Gretel, the first book, there is an ancient evil in the Back Country, dormant for centuries but now hungry and lurking.

When it sets its sights on an unsuspecting mother one routine morning along an isolated stretch of highway, a quiet farming family is suddenly thrust into a world of unspeakable terror, and a young girl must learn to be a hero.

Start reading Gretel today.[1]

To stay in touch with me, subscribe to my newsletter.[2]

---

1. https://www.amazon.com/Gretel-Christopher-Coleman-ebook/dp/B01605OOL4/

2. http://www.christophercolemanauthor.com/newsletter/

Made in the USA
Monee, IL
17 December 2020